AF271435

THORPE'S MAIL ORDER BRIDE

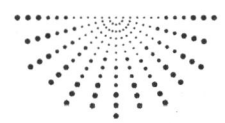

CYNTHIA WOOLF

Copyright © 2019 by Cynthia Woolf

All Rights Reserved. No part of this book may be reproduced or transmitted in any form or by any means, electrical, digital or mechanical including but not limited to photocopying, recording, scanning or by any type of data storage and retrieval system without express, written permission from the author.

Published by Firehouse Publishing
Woolf, Cynthia

Cover design copyright © 2021 Lori Jackson Design

CHAPTER ONE

*M*arch 1, 1887–New Orleans

*L*ena would never get used to the opulence of her mother's home. The mansion was not what she was used to back at the Oakfield School in Connecticut. She checked her hair in the mirror attached to the bureau in her room before heading downstairs for luncheon.

As she reached the end of the hall, a knock sounded on the front door. From the top of the curved staircase, Lena watched her mother's bald, a black butler, Thaddeus, answer the door.

"May I help you?" asked Thaddeus.

"I'm Robert Drummond. May I come in?"

She heard a man's voice and descended the stairs. A tall, powerfully built man with dark hair, graying at the temples, stood on the veranda, holding his black bowler hat. Beyond him she saw a horse-drawn carriage and the uniformed driver waiting at the bottom of the terraced walkway that was shaded by the large magnolia trees she so loved. She only wished it was later in the year for she missed their unique lemony smell.

"Miss Mellisande is not here at the moment. If you'll leave your card, I'll tell her you called."

"I didn't come to see Mellisande. I came to see Miss Helena DuBois."

"I'll deal with this man, Thaddeus. Thank you."

"Yes, Miss Helena."

The butler dipped his head and then left down the corridor.

Lena finished descending the stairs and then turned to the stranger.

With a raised eyebrow, she thought that formal name had never fit her, but she said, "I'm Helena DuBois, however I'm not in my mother's business. You'll have to come back later to see her." She tried to close the door, but he put his hand out stopping her.

"I'm not here for that kind of business, Helena. Please let me in so we aren't discussing this matter on the porch."

Porch. He was definitely from the North, but exactly where she couldn't discern from his accent.

Lena wasn't alone in the house, so she let the man in. "Very well. Follow me please."

She led the way to the library, down the hall

carpeted with thick oriental rugs. He followed her and closed the door behind them.

"Would you care to sit?"

She waved her hand toward the brocade upholstered sofa and green damask covered overstuffed chairs that stood in front of the fireplace. Lena loved the ornately hand-painted chintz draperies hanging on the tall windows that formed one wall of the room.

He sat in one damask chairs, and Lena sat in the other a long, low table between them.

"Helena, as I said my name is Robert Drummond and what I'm about to tell you will come as a shock. But your mother and I have talked and decided that it's time that you know."

He paused and took a deep breath.

"I'm your father."

Father. All this time she'd longed for a father. Had missed out on things like the father-daughter dances that the other girls at her school had attended. If she'd been standing, Lena might have collapsed. As it was, she simply tightened her hand on the padded chair arm and hoped the man couldn't see her shake within the chair. "That can't be. My mother would have told me if my father was alive."

"I can understand your reluctance to believe me, but it is the truth. I should have let Mellisande accompany me. She wanted to, you know, but I wanted to tell you myself, vain person that I am."

He turned his hat over and over on his lap.

"I thought sure you'd be happy about the news.

3

Look, I'm a well-known businessman and couldn't have my relationship with your mother known within certain circles. When you were two, we decided I should remarry and when you were six, we sent you away to school to shield you from your mother's business. One of your classmates, Eric Rappaport, is my stepson. Do you remember him?"

Lena's breath caught in her throat at that news. She sat straighter, glad she was sitting on the chair. "That's true," she nodded. "I do remember Eric. He was totally obnoxious and mean to me the whole time we were at school together. Does he know about this, too? That you're supposed to be my father."

Robert sat forward on his chair. "I'm afraid he does. He overheard me telling my wife, his mother, of your existence. I wanted to take care of you and did the best I could. Now, though, you're of an age that you must marry and have children of your own. I've found a suitable man back in New York. One of my business partners, actually. Your mother's association to you will never be known."

Anger gave Lena strength, and she stood, back straight. She would not show any softness toward him, no matter how much she wanted to have a father. He could be a complete liar. *But he wouldn't have known those things about me if he wasn't who he said he is.* "You propose to tell me that you're my father *and* I must marry someone you have chosen for me, all in few minutes. Are you out of your mind?"

"No. You are an adult now and need to take on adult responsibilities."

She couldn't believe his arrogance and she didn't need a stranger's help in securing a husband. She would remain calm, just like she did when the children she taught were getting rambunctious.

"I'll pick my own husband."

"Listen to me Helena—"

"My name is Lena and I refuse to be dictated to by a stranger. Please leave." She pulled the cord for Thaddeus.

The library door opened and Thaddeus entered. He was not just a butler, but also her mother's bodyguard. Lena had no fear when he was near. "You rang, Miss Lena?"

"Yes, Thaddeus. Please show out this *gentleman*."

"I'll leave now, Helena," Robert donned his hat. "But I'll be back in two weeks and I expect you to be ready to come with me to New York.

"Please leave, Mr. Drummond, before I have Thaddeus hail a police officer."

"As you wish." Drummond was not a happy man, but he stood and left through the door that Thaddeus held open. "I can find my own way out."

Lena shook all over. Never would she marry some man her mother, or her newly discovered father, had chosen for her. Her mother had tried before to get her to marry. Lena was shamed by Mellisande's business and might hate herself sometimes because of that shame, but she hadn't fallen so far that she would allow her mother to choose a husband for her. She hadn't before when Mellisande wanted her to, so why would her mother think that she would now? How could they tell her all of this at once and expect her to acquiesce to their demand? First she had a father, and second, she was supposed to marry some strange man, not of her choosing. That had been the problem last time. She hadn't chosen the man. Her mother had. This was no different and she would not stand for it.

She dropped into one of the large overstuffed chairs in front of the empty fireplace, making sure it was not the one her *father* had sat in. Grabbing the paper from the coffee table she flipped through the pages looking for a special advertisement. One she'd heard whispered about by her teacher friends at school when they wanted to marry.

Finally she found it and read to remind herself of the details.

Women wanted. Matchmaker & Co in Golden, Colorado is recruiting women with the object of marriage to one of their thoroughly screened bachelors. These men are farmers, ranchers, miners, and of other occupations that are desirous of marriage and family. Contact Mrs. Maggie Black, with your photograph and the type of man you are looking for.

This was perfect. She could choose a husband far away from both New York and New Orleans. Her parents would never find her and she'd finally lead her own life as she saw fit.

Rather than write Mrs. Black, she would go to

Golden and visit the office directly. She had the money saved, almost one thousand dollars. That would see her through until she got to her husband, whoever he might be.

She was only visiting Mellisande and did not feel any allegiance to her mother to let her know she was leaving. In fact that was the last thing she wanted to do. She packed two valises—one with everyday dresses, and one with under garments, perfume, hankies, and anything else she could cram inside.

Her feeling of elation was odd. She was finally making her own decisions. And it felt good.

She quietly left the house carrying the bags and without alerting the servants. Then she hailed a cab and directed the driver to take her to the train station. There she purchased the tickets for the five-day trip that would get her to Golden. The train wouldn't be leaving for several hours.

After she got her tickets, she bought three box lunches from a woman selling them for fifty cents each. She got a paper bag from another vendor for a nickel. She carefully put the apples, cheese and chicken sandwiches into the bag, along with two loaves of bread she'd bought from another woman for a quarter. There were many people selling food and water at the station. They knew the train didn't stop for hours and there was no dining car on most of the trains she would be riding on.

Finally the train was ready for boarding and Lena made her way to the conductor with her ticket and baggage.

"Would you like to check those bags, miss?" asked the conductor as he took her ticket.

"Oh, no thank you. I'm changing trains several times and in the interest of expediency, I'll keep them with me." She wanted to be able to leave and run anytime she needed to. Constantly keeping vigil for anyone that looked like they might have been sent by her mother and following her.

He smiled. "Very well, miss."

Lena took the Southern Pacific Railroad to Ft. Worth, Texas, where she changed to the Union Pacific Railroad to Denver. From there she rode the Colorado Central Railroad into Golden.

She saw landscapes unlike anything she'd ever seen in Connecticut and certainly not in New Orleans, from the lush foliage of New Orleans, the prairie of Texas might as well have been desert, and then through the New Mexico Territory, traveling along the rolling countryside with mountains to the west and prairie to the east. When she reached Golden, nestled against the foothills of the Rocky Mountains, she thought she might have entered a different but beautiful country. The town itself was small but bustling with farmers, ranchers and miners from the gold mines to the west in Central City.

It took her five full days to travel from New Orleans to Golden, where she arrived on March 6th. Lena was so tired and sore from sitting up while trying to sleep and not being able to change clothes at all during the trip.

Her corset felt as though it had melded with her skin and she was almost afraid to take it off.

She found Matchmaker & Co's offices and entered a room that was sparsely furnished. Lena set her bags against the wall just inside the door. The room contained a desk in the center, file cabinets behind the desk, a potbellied stove in the right corner of the rear wall with a pot of coffee emitting the heavenly smell that assaulted her when she entered. A door was situated in the left corner of the same wall.

Windows on either side of the bright blue front door lent light to the room, as did a window on the wall to her left. A lovely redheaded woman with vibrant green eyes glanced at the bags Lena left by the door and then came forward her hand extended in greeting.

"Are you Mrs. Black?" Lena shook the offered hand.

"Yes, I'm Maggie Black. Please come in and sit. Where have you traveled from Miss…"

Lena sat and was glad to have finally arrived at her destination. "DuBois. Helena DuBois, but everyone calls me Lena."

"Very well, Lena. Where are you from?"

"I've come from New Orleans and I'm looking for a husband. I spent the last five years teaching at The Oakbridge School in Connecticut. I left that position at the end of last term and was visiting my mother in New Orleans. I do have references from the school if you would like to see them."

"In a moment. You appear to have come here directly

from the train. Wouldn't you like to refresh yourself and have a cup of coffee and perhaps a cookie? You must be famished. I know what the food at those train stops are like, unless you happen to get to a Harvey House."

"Actually, I did visit one in Albuquerque. The restaurant was wonderful. The food was hot and delicious and they served it fast so we didn't miss the train."

"Good. Now I have coffee and molasses cookies that I'm sure will please you."

Lena eyed the coffee pot on the potbellied stove and thought of the cookies. Her mouth began to water. "Yes, I would love both. Do you have someplace where I can clean up and remove the last two days of ashes and other grime?"

"Certainly. A bathroom is behind that door. Help yourself." Mrs. Black pointed at a bright blue door that matched the entry one. Inside was a sink with a water pump, a stack of washcloths, and a towel. In the corner was a hamper for the used linen. "The outhouse is out back," called Mrs. Black.

Lena returned shortly after having washed her hands and face. For the first time in days, she felt truly refreshed.

Mrs. Black sat behind her desk reading something in a folder that she closed when Lena returned.

"Please sit, Miss DuBois." She pointed at the wooden chair in front of her desk. "Now, why are you looking to be a mail-order bride? Honesty will serve best here, that way I can help you find your best match."

Lena told her the whole story. She didn't even leave out the shameful fact that her mother ran a bordello or that it was the most famous house of ill repute in New Orleans.

"I see. Well, Lena, I believe I can help you. I have several men that could be a good match. There is a farmer in Kansas and a rancher in Colorado, but I also have a blacksmith in Homestead Canyon, in the Wyoming Territory, who I think would be perfect. His name is John Thorpe. Here is his photograph."

She handed Lena a tintype picture of a man with dark hair and beard. He wore a dark suit jacket and pants with a white shirt and held a hat with a wide brim and flat crown.

Mrs. Black reached in the folder and brought out a single sheet of paper. "He is looking for a woman of good moral character. I believe that is you. You've avoided your mother's business and are refusing to be chattel for your father. I personally like that."

"Mrs. Black, thank you. I don't know what I would have done without you."

"Call me Maggie. You're a resourceful woman. You would have found a solution. But I have to ask… you're fleeing a marriage to one unknown man and pursuing marriage with another. Why?"

"Because this is *my* choice. I'm not having anyone foisted on me. At least I've seen Mr. Thorpe and your company has checked him out. I know he's not going to abuse me and he's not a drunkard. I know more about him than I do the man my *father*, assuming he was telling the truth, wanted me to marry."

"Very well." Maggie leaned her elbows on her desk and steepled her fingers. "I'll inform Mr. Thorpe that you will be coming his way. I suggest you purchase appropriate clothing before you leave. You'll need clothes for cold weather. A good wool coat, boots, wool dresses, skirts and blouses. As well as boots for the winter you'll need sturdy leather boots for everyday wear when there is no snow on the ground. Would you care to write Mr. Thorpe yourself? He has sent a bank draft that will cover your train tickets to Hanover in the Wyoming Territory. He will meet you there where you will marry. Then the trip to Homestead Canyon is two days ride from there."

"Oh, yes, please. I would love to write Mr. Thorpe."

Maggie got a pen, ink and paper out of one of her desk drawers.

"Here you go. Compose your letter. I'll post it with mine.

"Thank you."

*M*arch 6, 1887
Dear Mr. Thorpe:

My name is Helena DuBois. I am twenty-three years old. I was raised in Connecticut, consider myself to be of high moral character and am looking for that attribute in the man that I marry. As to my background, my father is a very successful New York businessman and well respected.

Having just finished five years as a teacher at the boarding school I attended from the time I was six, I am now ready for a home and family of my own.

A man of equally high standards as my own, is the person I seek to marry and you, I believe, are that person. I want someone who would help to raise any children we have in a moral and Godly manner.

To that end, I accept your proposal of marriage and will travel to Homestead Canyon after I make a few purchases for our new home. I also must get clothing more in line with the weather there. I understand that your winters and springs can be quite cold. I've been in New Orleans for the last six months and it may take me some time to acclimate myself again to the cold and snow.

Mrs. Black has told me that I can take the train to Hanover, which she tells me is the closest I can get to Homestead Canyon. It is my understanding we will be married in Hanover before leaving on the two-day journey by wagon to Homestead Canyon, to our home.

I look forward to meeting you and to the beginning of our life together.

Sincerely,

Lena DuBois

She read over the letter, sanded it and then handed it to Maggie Black for posting.

Maggie added Lena's letter to the envelope she'd addressed to Mr. Thorpe.

I'm very glad for my savings. I'll need to spend some of it on new, warmer clothes since I left most of my wardrobe packed in crates at mother's. I also want to purchase things for the house to make it more homey. "Where can I buy clothing and perhaps some things for the house? I most definitely need a heavier coat and a traveling suit. I do have money, so that won't be a problem."

"My letter will take approximately ten days to get to Mr. Thorpe and another ten days for his response to be returned. I suggest renting a room at the Astor House here in Golden and then take the horse drawn-trolley or the train back to Denver and shop at the Denver Dry Goods, Co. They will have everything you need."

"Thank you. I will."

Lena had all of her savings, more than one thousand dollars. She had one hundred in her reticule, another four hundred in cash, sewn into the hem of her favorite pink dress and the rest, five hundred and seventy-one dollars in the form of a bank draft in the bottom of her valise.

First, she found the Astor House and took a room for the next three weeks. The first thing she did was order a bath. Having a hot bath for the first time in days felt like a luxury. After her bath, she realized she was exhausted. She knew she should dress and go out for dinner, but sleep sounded ever so much better. Putting on her night-gown she crawled between the cool, white sheets and was asleep almost as soon as her head hit the pillow.

The next morning she felt revived and ready to greet

the world. She had breakfast in a nearby restaurant and walked back to the train station to board the train for Denver. The horse-drawn trolley would take about two hours to get to Denver from Golden whereas the train would only take twenty minutes. She wanted as much time as possible to shop and make her choices. Lena knew that she'd have to live with them for a long time.

The store was in the middle of town on Sixteenth and California streets. Excited, Lena loved to shop, but shopping with purpose was best. She thought her shopping trip would likely take a good chunk of the money she'd saved. She intended to buy clothes for every occasion and books. She couldn't do without some of her favorite novels. What else would she do at night after dinner? She didn't know how to knit or crochet, just didn't have the patience that was needed to do the job well.

She wore the heavy wool coat, gloves and fur hat out of the store along with the warm rabbit fur-lined boots. The rest she put in the trunks and arranged for their delivery to the Astor house.

The boarding house was quite nice and, she thought, very reasonably priced. The owner of the establishment had installed a bathtub and charged everyone, boarders or not, twenty-five cents per bath. A room rented for one dollar and fifty cents per day and included meals. It was rumored that the owner made more profit from the bathtub than the room rentals.

Lena constantly looked over her shoulder. Fear gripped her whenever she left the Astor House. What if they found her before she could leave for Homestead Canyon? The longer she stayed here the more likely her father or mother could find her, assuming they were actually looking. Regardless, she wanted to be gone and get to Wyoming.

Back at the boarding house, Lena admitted she was excited to meet Mr. Thorpe. Mrs. Black had given her the letter he'd written asking for a bride. In it he described himself, though Lena knew from the photograph that he was a handsome man. According to his letter he had black hair and blue eyes, all his teeth and good eyesight. He was a blacksmith by trade, owned his own business and home and was looking for a wife of good moral character.

Lena knew she was of good moral character. Her parents might not be, but Lena was. She was not her mother. That was the one good thing Mellisande had done. By sending away Lena, she kept the stigma of the bordello from reaching her daughter.

---

*L*ena's time at the Astor House was almost up. She supposed she could go to a day-by-day rental, but she'd rather know when she was taking the train to the Wyoming Territory.

Finally, Maggie Black sent for her.

Lena put on her coat and boots and hurried down the hill to the office.

"We've gotten a response from Mr. Thorpe. He would like it very much if you would marry him."

Maggie handed Lena the missive.

The handwriting was very nice as was the first one. Unusual she thought, because every other man she knew had terrible handwriting.

Lena pressed the letter to her chest and grinned at Maggie.

"You did it, Maggie. He wants me. I'll soon be Mrs. John Thorpe."

"Lena," Maggie said gently. "I know I shouldn't be asking this as it will sound like I'm discouraging business, but my curiosity has gotten the better of me. Why didn't you just go to another town and start a new life? You're a beautiful woman. Why I know women who would kill to have the pale blonde hair and blue eyes like yours."

"I want to be married. I want to be wanted and John already wants me. More than anything I need to be far enough away from New Orleans that my mother will never find me. No one who knows her would ever go to a place like Homestead Canyon. I'll be safe."

---

*M*arch 8, 1887–The DuBois Mansion – New Orleans

. . .

"Mellisande, my love, come back to bed."

From where she stood at the window, she looked over at Robert. He was the most vibrant person she knew. Strong and robust and hers. "I cannot darling. Our Helena is out there somewhere. Alone."

"I should have waited and told her with you present. I scared her with talk of a marriage and telling her I'm her father. The information was too much all at once. This entire situation is my fault. I've hired the Pinkerton Detective Agency to find her. If anyone can they will."

Mellisande stepped away from the window and walked back to the bed.

Robert held up the blankets.

She crawled in, scooting next to him and cuddled into his warmth. "Do you think Helena will believe we got married six years ago? She'll wonder why we didn't tell her."

"We are only trying to protect her, from the vicious gossip that would have ensued if we told anyone."

"I know that, but will our daughter see it that way? She is very resentful of me and what I do. She will wonder why I continue my business."

"Something I have asked you many times before."

She leaned up and turned to look at his face. "You know that I won't be dependent on anyone, including you, my love. I protect my girls, and I won't abandon them."

He hugged her.

"I understand, but that doesn't mean I'll stop asking you to sell it and move to New York."

"You could always leave New York and move to New Orleans."

He laughed. "For the past thirty years, we have this conversation every time I'm here. It's a good thing I love you."

"And I you." She rested against his chest, her fingers curling in the dusting of hair. "When will you know about Helena?"

"It could be as soon as next week and maybe not for months. It will depend on how much our daughter wishes to hide. She's a smart woman."

"I feared you would say that."

Mellisande could not hold back her tears. "I'm so afraid for her. She is very naïve. She's never been out in the world alone, always sheltered by the school."

"I know but she is our daughter. She will be fine and when we find her we'll bring her home."

"I hope so." She rested against him and couldn't help but worry for her only child.

CHAPTER TWO

*A*pril 14, 1887

*B*ig John Thorpe, patted along the horse's side as he walked to her rear. He didn't want to surprise her and get kicked. Luckily, old Bessie was well used to having new shoes put on. All he had to do was touch the roan's fetlock to get her to raise her hoof. John bent his knee and supported the hoof on his calf while he filed, sanded, and scraped the hoof in preparation for the shoe.

When he was done with Bessie, he could leave for Hanover to get his bride, Miss Helena DuBois. He still couldn't believe he would be a married man two days from now.

He'd already had a talk with Reverend Ritter the last time he conducted church services in Homestead

Canyon. John asked if he would perform the ceremony when his bride arrived in Hanover. The good reverend had said doing so wouldn't be a problem at all. He was always happy to wed members of the community.

Now if only this snow would let up. He could ride through it, but his new wife wouldn't be very happy riding home in a blizzard. He made sure to pack plenty of blankets to keep her warm. She was from the South. New Orleans, Louisiana to be exact and definitely was not used to cold weather, much less deep snow. He knew she would acclimate, but not all in one day.

---

*A*pril 16, 1887

*L*ena was definitely the worse for wear. She'd remembered for this part of her journey to bring along a washcloth to clean her face and hands at each stop where she was able. That was something she hadn't done on the trip from New Orleans to Denver, and she'd been miserable. Her hair and coat were coated with dirt and ash by the time she arrived in Hanover. But the washcloth, while making her more presentable, didn't eliminate the discomfort of riding on the train for days, while wearing a corset that restricted her breathing and a bustle that made sitting for long periods uncomfortable.

The engineer blew the whistle at each stop.

The shrill sound traveled up her spine and gave her a headache. This time, however, the stop was hers and she didn't have to stay on the train. Today she'd meet and marry Mr. John Thorpe. She'd done very well by keeping on her heavy black wool coat; her navy traveling suit had remained relatively clean. She hoped there would be somewhere to change into a nice dress before getting married, but she wasn't sure and so was prepared to marry in her blue suit.

The train came to a stop, and the conductor came through calling, "Hanover. Hanover."

He stopped and smiled at Lena.

"This is your destination, Miss DuBois."

Lena stood and swayed a little as the train slowed, the brakes letting out a squeal. She grabbed her valise and her parasol from the overhead bin.

"Thank you, Mr. Crane. You've been very kind to me."

He tipped his hat in her direction.

"Just doing my job, miss."

Lena's stomach turned over, and she placed her hand on top of her belly to still the sensation. She shuddered at the cold air and adjusted her scarf to pull it up to her chin. Then she walked back to the door and down the steps to the train platform.

A man unloaded her trunks and set them on the platform.

She stood by the trunks, her valise sitting on top of one, her umbrella point on the ground.

The street was covered with a blanket of new snow. She waited for an hour inside the train depot for Mr. Thorpe, walking back and forth in front of the station to keep an eye on the door. Finally, deciding he was either not coming or had been seriously delayed she went to talk to the stationmaster.

"Excuse me. Can you tell me if there is a hotel in town?"

"No hotel, miss, but the Johnson's rent out their spare room to those in need of a place to stay. I'll give you directions. You can leave your trunks here. No one will disturb them."

"Thank you, sir. That is very kind of you."

The stationmaster blushed and waved off her thanks.

The Johnson's lived at the other end of town and the walk seemed very long with the wind pushing against her.

Lena walked past the saloon just as a man stumbled out.

He leaned against the side of the building for a minute.

She knew the moment he saw her.

He got a wide grin on his face, straightened from the wall and ambled over to her. "Well, hello there, girlie. You got a little kiss for old Barney, hmmm?"

The drunken man raised his arms to envelope Lena.

She raised her parasol, poked the man in the stomach, and then hit him over the head with the umbrella.

"Stay away, you stupid man. I am not some doxie to be pawed by the likes of you."

Raising the parasol she beat off the drunken man. With her last blow, the umbrella broke.

He retreated back inside the saloon from whence he came.

"Are you all right, my dear?"

A gray-haired woman with kind blue eyes and dressed in a gray coat with a black shawl layered over the garment, hurried forward.

"Did he hurt you?"

Lena tugged at the sleeves on her coat and checked her hat. "No, ma'am. I'm fine. The sot thought I was some sort of saloon girl just because I was passing in front of the establishment."

"Where are you headed, miss?"

Lena held out her hand. "Lena DuBois. I'm going to the Johnsons. I've been told that they rent out a spare room."

The woman took Lena's hand. "I'm Mrs. Ritter. My husband is the minister here. Who were you supposed to meet?"

As far as Lena was concerned, she couldn't have run in to a better person to know the whereabouts of her husband. "Mr. John Thorpe. He's my husband... er... he will be as soon as we wed. I'm a mail-order bride and have come here to marry Mr. Thorpe. I assume your husband will be doing the ceremony."

"Oh, I'm sure John's just delayed. We had this spring snow yesterday and the roads to Homestead Canyon can become difficult to travel. I'm sure he'll be here as soon as possible. Now rather than stand out here in the cold, why don't you come home with me? Surely once he realizes you are not at the depot, he'll come to our house straight away."

Lena's shoulders relaxed and relief washed through her. "Thank you, Mrs. Ritter. Your offer is very kind."

"Nonsense. Come along."

Mrs. Ritter took Lena by the elbow and they walked toward the end of the street and the tall church steeple.

Traveling through the snow, a good eight inches on the ground, causing her to lift the front of her skirt to travel through the cold, white powder, lengthened the duration of the walk to the small white house next to the church. By the time they reached the home, Lena was frozen and very grateful for the warmth she felt as she followed Mrs. Ritter inside.

"Come now, hang your coat on one of the pegs by the door. I'm glad to see you brought sensible clothing."

"Yes, I made many purchases in Denver, Colorado, before I worked my way north. But this last leg of the train ride, with no padding on the wooden seat, was the worst. I basically sat on a wooden bench for three days while the train wound its way north from Cheyenne."

"You probably don't want to sit after that. If you'll follow me to the living room, you'll find a roaring fire and soft chairs that you will find inviting. I'll make us some tea."

Lena followed the woman, who was a couple of inches taller than her own five-feet-two height.

The room was indeed very nice with the fire blazing in the hearth. A comfortable-looking sofa covered in a flowery green material sat in front of the fireplace with two matching overstuffed chairs on either end. A low table was situated in front of the couch.

"This is very nice of you Mrs. Ritter. Won't Mr. Thorpe be looking for me at either the train station or the Johnson's?"

"He'll come here when he doesn't find you at either of those places, don't worry. Hanover isn't that big. If I know John, he'll knock on every door until he finds you. Now make yourself at home, and I'll get the tea."

Mrs. Ritter hurried away.

Lena settled herself on the divan. The piece was *very* comfortable. This was the most relaxed she'd been since leaving Golden.

With a sigh, she rested against the back of the sofa and closed her eyes.

"Wake up, my dear. Wake up."

Mrs. Ritter patted Lena's cheeks.

Oh goodness! She'd fallen asleep. "Forgive me Mrs. Ritter. Your settee is wonderfully soft and my body needed the rest after the long train ride and no sleep."

"That's fine, dear. I only woke you because John is here and waiting in the kitchen to meet his bride."

"Oh my." She sat up straight. Suddenly the butterflies were back in her stomach at the news. "I must look a mess. Do you have any place for me to freshen myself?"

"Certainly, come with me."

Mrs. Ritter led the way to a bedroom.

"Here we are. I'll be back in a few minutes."

Lena looked at her reflection in the small mirror over the washstand. Patting her hair into place, she turned and gazed around the room. The furnishings were austere in the extreme. With the bit of furniture present the space was all but used. In addition to the washstand was a simple four-poster with a patchwork quilt and a bureau. Pegs fastened to the wall held various items of clothing.

A few minutes later, Mrs. Ritter returned with a copper kettle, the handle of which was wrapped with a towel. She poured hot water into the basin and cooler water from the chipped rose-patterned pitcher from the bureau.

"The towels next to the ewer are clean. When you've finished washing, come meet your groom. I sent him next door to get my husband. We'll get you two married shortly."

"Married? I know we are supposed to marry right away but thought we might get to know each other for a few hours."

"That won't be possible. He has to return to his business in Homestead Canyon right away. Unless, of course, accompany him now and marry in a couple of weeks." Mrs. Ritter frowned. "But I don't think you'd want to take that action. Your reputation, which you so diligently defended little more than an hour ago, would be ruined."

Lena swallowed hard. A marriage and changing her name was the best way to stay hidden. "Well then," She jutted her chin. "Let's get this wedding started."

She followed Mrs. Ritter back to the parlor.

Dominating the room was the largest man Lena had ever seen. He was easily a foot taller than she was and very wide, though he did not appear to be fat. He wore a black suit, the same one as in the photograph he'd sent. His face was covered with a thick, well-trimmed beard and mustache, though his coal black hair was a little on the long side, as it curled over his collar, but his deep blue eyes caught her attention. They were not only a beautiful dark blue, but she saw kindness in them as well.

The man moved forward to greet her, and Lena was surprised at how graceful he was.

He extended his hand. "I'm John Thorpe."

She grasped his hand, calloused from hard work. "Lena DuBois. Pleased to meet you."

"And I you. I'm sorry I was late. The snow delayed me."

Lena nodded. "Mrs. Ritter said as much."

"Would you like to get married now, Lena?"

"I'm ready. I understand you have to get back to your work."

John worried the brim of his hat. "Yes, I do. I'm the only blacksmith in town and folks do depend on me. But we can sit and talk for a while before the ceremony if that would make you more comfortable."

She shook her head. *He was so sweet to make such an offer.* "No, please, that's fine. I'm ready to get married if you are. I didn't come all this way to back out now."

He smiled. "I'm very glad, Lena. Very glad indeed."

"Sit down, children." Mrs. Ritter pointed at the sofa.

Lena sat on one end and smoothed her skirts.

John sat on the other end. He held his hat in his hands between his knees.

"You are getting quite the feisty woman for your bride, John. I witnessed her defend her honor a short while ago when she was accosted by a drunk from the saloon." Mrs. Ritter then relayed everything she'd seen.

John grinned and arched an eyebrow. "Good for you Miss DuBois."

Lena's cheeks heated, and she dipped her head. "I was simply doing what any self-respecting young woman would have done."

"No, that's not true," said John. "You saved yourself and didn't wait to be saved by someone else. Not a lot of women would have beaten off their attacker with an umbrella."

"That reminds me, John," said Mrs. Ritter. "You must buy her a new umbrella. She broke hers over that drunks head."

Reverend Ritter entered the living room.

"Ah, I see everyone is here. Are you two ready to get married?"

Lena and John looked at each other.

"Well?" asked John.

"I'm ready if you are," responded Lena.

John stood and walked to the reverend.

The men shook hands.

"We are ready, Reverend."

Mrs. Ritter and Lena both stood as well.

"I think we can do the ceremony right here. Lena, you and John stand behind the sofa and the Reverend will stand in front of it. I'll be over here just behind Lena."

The couple did as Mrs. Ritter instructed.

The reverend took out a small notebook and a pencil from his pocket. "Before we start, I need to know your full names."

"Helena Marguerite DuBois."

"John Wilfred Thorpe."

"Wilfred?" Lena giggled.

John smiled and blushed. "It was my grandfather's name."

Lena nodded. "Marguerite was my grandmother's name. It would appear we have the same traditions, at least as far as naming children."

The reverend opened the good book and began the ceremony.

"Please join hands. Dearly beloved we are gathered here…"

Soon Lena's turn to take her vows arrived.

"Do you Helena Marguerite DuBois, take John Wilfred Thorpe, to be thy wedded husband, to have and to hold, from this day forward, for better, for worse, for richer, for poorer, in sickness and in health, to love and to cherish, till death do you part, according to God's holy ordinance; and thereto pledge to forsake all others?"

Excitement ran through her like a lightning bolt. "I

do." She put the ring she'd bought in Denver on John's finger. The circle of gold went up to the second knuckle and stopped. Eyes wide, she looked up at him. "Oh, my." Quickly she took the ring off his third finger and slid it on his little finger. It fit. "That will have to do until we can get is sized correctly."

The reverend repeated the vows for John who answered "I do." He put on the plain gold band he had for her and it was too big.

She took it off and put it on her middle finger, which fit the ring perfectly. "That will do, don't you think?" asked Lena with a smile.

John grinned. "I believe it will."

Reverend Ritter smiled. "You may now kiss your bride."

John's grin disappeared, and he studied her face. He bent until his face was next to hers and then touched his lips to hers in a sweet, gentle kiss.

Her first kiss.

When he pulled back, he winked.

She started to laugh but stifled it and smiled instead.

John turned to the reverend. "Thank you. I appreciate you making yourself available for us." He handed Reverend Ritter a five-dollar gold piece. "For the church."

"Thank you, John. The gesture is appreciated though not required."

The two men shook hands again.

Mrs. Ritter hugged Lena. "If you have any questions

about anything…" She rolled her eyes toward John. "You just let me know."

Lena lowered her gaze to the floor. "I think we'll be fine," she whispered.

She wasn't about to tell sweet Mrs. Ritter that she knew exactly what was supposed to happen on her wedding night. That was something her mother had not kept secret. She was well aware what sex was, though tonight—or one night in the future if she could convince John to wait—would be her first experience with the age-old dance between a man and a woman.

Reverend Ritter nodded. "I wish you both a very happy marriage blessed with many children."

Now was John's turn to blush. "Uh, yes, so do I."

Lena nodded and shifted her gaze back to the floor.

Mrs. Ritter handed John a basket.

"This is for your trip. I hope I've packed enough for today and tomorrow."

John took the basket. "Thank you, Mrs. Ritter. This is very kind of you." Then he held out his arm to Lena. "Shall we? We've got a long drive ahead, and I'd like to reach one of the wayfarer cabins before nightfall."

She fitted her small hand into the crook of his arm. Another trip. Two more days sitting on a hard bench, but then she'd be home. Her home. Their home. "Then let's go… husband."

John grinned, "Wife." He moved toward the door. "Thank you again, Reverend," he called over his shoulder.

They crunched through the snow to the wagon. Lena

let go of his arm and began to climb up the side of the wagon to the bench. Suddenly John's hands were there on her waist and she was flying as he lifted her into the buckboard.

Lena straightened her skirts. "I know most husbands don't lift their wives into the wagon. I think you did that just so you could touch me."

John laughed. "Guilty. That's exactly why I did it."

He climbed up next to her, picked up the reins and slapped them hard on the horses' rumps.

The wagon lurched forward as the animals began to walk.

"The drive's a sixteen hour trip with the wagon to Homestead Canyon. You and I will do it in two days. We'll get your trunks from the train depot and then stop at one of the wayfarer cabins tonight. Blankets are stowed under the seat to keep you warm. Luckily the snow has stopped. I'd like to reach the farthest cabin, but I doubt we'll make it that far. We've got a bit of a late start this morning what with the wedding and all."

The wind blew, brisk and icy, and Lena buttoned up her coat, reaching for a thick, woolen blanket from beneath the seat. "Well, the cause of our late start, 'the wedding and all' is the only way this trip could be made. Otherwise you'd be traveling on your own."

"Point taken." John nodded.

*A*pril 25, 1887 – The Drummond mansion, New York City

"*R*obert, my darling, what can I do for you? How can I make you more comfortable?"

He put his arm out to the side. "Come lie with me."

Mellisande quickly unknotted the belt on her robe and climbed in next to her husband.

"You cannot die on me, Robert. You've been my friend and my lover for thirty years. How can I go on without you?"

He brought his other arm around and squeezed her. Then he rested. The simple act of holding her seemed to be too much for him to do.

"You will go on because you must think of Helena. The Pinkerton Detective came to see me today, as you know. He believes he's found Helena. She has married and moved to a place in the Wyoming Territory called Homestead Canyon. He has taken so long to find any trace of her, I was afraid he would not do so before I depart this earth."

"Do not talk like that. You still have to talk with Helena. She needs to know you before she can accept you are her father." She closed her eyes.

"This is my fault. I should have arranged for you and I to go together when I met her for the first time. She would not be gone from us, from you, if not for me."

"Nonsense. Everything will be fine. We'll go see Helena together and meet her husband. All will be well."

"I'm afraid my love, that I'm past that. I won't get to see our Helena again. You will have to tell her about me. Let her know that I always loved her. From the moment she was born, I loved her."

Tears rolled down Mellisande's cheeks. She leaned up on her elbow and smoothed Robert's hair.

"You will tell her yourself. When you get better, you'll tell her."

"My darling, Mellisande, I wish I'd married you sooner. I'm sorry for all the time we missed because of our misplaced morality. I love you more today than yesterday. More than I have anyone ever."

"Oh Robert. I too love you. I'm sorry I didn't accept your proposal long ago."

"Hold me, Mellisande. Hold me."

"Robert. Robert."

Only silence greeted her. Robert was gone.

"Oh, my love. How will I survive without you?"

She laid her head on his chest and let the tears flow.

---

*E*ric Rappaport paced the library, waiting for the doctor to come down from tending to Robert. The whore, Mellisande DuBois, was upstairs, but the physician didn't want Eric there.

Robert was dying. No doubt existed about that now.

He'd brought Mellisande from New Orleans a month ago and wouldn't have done so otherwise.

Eric knew Robert had been sick—in fact he'd made sure of it with arsenic he'd been giving the older man in his nightly brandy. Robert looked robust enough, since he'd returned from New Orleans one month ago, but now he was dying. Finally.

Why he brought *her* Eric didn't know. Maybe he was simply tired of their affair being hidden. As long as they didn't marry before Robert died, Eric was fine with whatever they wanted to do. Just so nothing interfered with his inheritance from Robert.

He needed that money. His credit was extended as far as he could manage. His creditors waited, not so patiently, for Robert to die.

Eric had done as much as he could to aid Robert's demise. Now that Robert was definitely dying, Mellisande wouldn't let Eric prepare him anything. She made all of Robert's after-dinner drinks herself. Eric was surprised she wasn't acting as food tester.

He took a large swallow from the snifter he held. Even the best brandy burned his throat on the way down. This was his special brandy… the stuff without the arsenic. The sound of the door opening behind him caused him to turn.

Mellisande stood there, seeming much taller than her five-foot-two-inch stature.

"He's gone, Eric. Robert has died."

While he rejoiced inside, he closed his eyes and let a tear fall. "Oh, my God. I had hoped against hope he would pull through." He approached Mellisande with his arms out ready to give her a comforting hug. As he got closer he noticed her eyes were red from crying, but she narrowed them when she looked at him. The look was hard and calculating.

"I don't know exactly how you did it, but I know you killed Robert. If I could prove it I'd call the police and have you arrested. But I can't. The doctor will inform the authorities of Robert's passing and he knows of my suspicions. I want them on record."

Eric stopped cold, dropping his arms to his side. "Mellisande, I don't know what I've done to make you think that I could have murdered Robert. I did not, I assure you. I would have to be insane to want to kill the man who supported me all my life. Without Robert, I don't know what I would have done. He meant a lot to me." *Yes, ten million is a lot. And now, I'm the one who will inherit.*

"The coroner will arrive to pick Robert up and take him to the mortuary. We'll have to arrange for a memorial service and notify all of his friends and business partners."

"Why are you making these arrangements? I appreciate your help, but it is not necessary for you to be here any longer."

"I've sent a note to Jacob Goldstein, Robert's attorney. He'll arrange for the reading of Robert's will. I'm sure there will be surprises for both of us."

Eric lifted an indolent eyebrow. "What surprises

could there be? I am Robert's heir and the only legitimate child."

She tossed her head back and straightened to her full height. "You may be legitimate, but you aren't Robert's child. Your mother made sure that you retained the Rappaport name. Robert wanted to adopt you, but she refused."

He'd never known that. What was his mother thinking leaving him with his ne'r-do-well father's name?

"What does that have to do with anything? I'm still his son, his heir."

"We'll see when Jacob comes tomorrow, won't we?"

Eric narrowed his eyes. "What do you mean? What do you know, Mellisande?" She knew something she wasn't saying, and it wasn't that she knew he'd poisoned Robert. No, she knew something else. Did Robert leave her his estate? No. He wouldn't do that. Even Robert couldn't have been that infatuated. He wouldn't have put his businesses at risk… for a whore. Eric was the one who would take care of Robert's various business interests. He was the one who Robert trusted to be on the board of the steel mill.

A small voice in his head said that was only so he could keep an eye on you.

"Did you say the reading of the will is tomorrow? Why so quick?"

"Robert wanted it that way. He wanted his estate settled as quickly as possible."

"That's fine with me. The sooner the document is read, the sooner I can throw you out."

Mellisande turned on her heel then stopped at the door and faced Eric. "We shall see who will be throwing out whom, won't we?" Exiting into the hall, she let the door slam shut.

"What in the world did she mean by that?" he asked the empty room.

*A*pril 26, 1887

*J*acob Goldstein arrived at the appointed hour and was shown to the library where Mellisande and Eric awaited.

Mellisande rose from the leather armchair and walked across the thick carpet to greet the man.

"Jacob. It's good to see you. I wish the reason was not such a sad occasion."

"I, too, wish the same. Robert will be missed. Shall I take the chair behind the desk?"

"Yes, please. Eric and I are already seated in front."

"How are you, Eric?" Jacob asked as he sat in the large dark leather chair.

"I'm fine... uh... considering the sad nature of your visit." Eric thought he should add this last so he seemed remorseful rather than excited by Jacob's appearance.

Jacob opened his case. He removed a folder and placed it on the desk in front of him. He then took an envelope out of the folder and removed two sheets of paper.

Holding up the document, he began to read. *"This is the last will and testament of Robert James Drummond."* He read almost a dozen bequests to the staff. Then he looked up. "The next part is of particular interest in that it pertains to both of you."

"To Mellisande DuBois, the love of my life, I leave two hundred and fifty thousand dollars and the mansion on Drummond Drive."

"No," Eric shouted and pushed to a rigid stand. "What am I supposed to do if you own this house?"

"Now, please sit again, Eric. I'm not finished," Jacob instructed.

Eric sat and waited. If the old man had left Mellisande that much, then Eric should get the rest of the estate. He began to relax. He pulled on the high starched collar of his shirt with a finger and loosened a bit, he felt he could breathe again.

"To Eric Rappaport, I leave my hunting lodge outside Albany and the apartment in New York along with a yearly stipend of ten thousand dollars."

"What?" Eric jumped to his feet, blood pounding in his ears. The creditors would kill him. "How can he leave me only that? What happens to the rest of his money?"

"Sit *down*, Eric, so I can finish," demanded Mr. Goldstein.

Eric sat, bouncing his knee in frustration, his hands clenched in fists on his thighs.

"The remainder of my estate I leave to my only child, Helena DuBois Drummond. She may do with the money as she sees fit. I've instructed my attorney, Mr. Jacob Goldstein, to find Helena and sell off all the business interests, leaving only a cash estate of approximately ten million dollars."

"Helena! He's leaving all that money to a bastard."

Mellisande turned to Eric and slapped his face. "Do not call my child a bastard."

"Well she is. You and Robert were not married."

She narrowed her gaze. "You are wrong. We married six years ago, two years after your mother's death. Due to his business interests *and mine*, we chose to keep the marriage a secret, but it is valid. Jacob has all the paperwork in his file."

"No." Eric's hand fisted again and he wailed. "This can't be happening."

Jacob put the documents back in the folder and returned it to his case. "She is correct. This will was made six years ago when he added his wife, Mellisande DuBois as Mrs. Drummond, to the recipients."

"I'll take the will to court, have it overturned."

"No court in the country will overturn this document." Mr. Goldstein slammed his fist on the desk. "If anything the judge would take your bequest and give it back to Mellisande. She was his legal wife and upon their marriage, Helena became their legitimate daughter. You, on the other hand, are no blood relation at all.

Robert leaving you anything was a kindness as far as I'm concerned, and I advised against it. But he said he'd supported you all these years and you had nothing to fall back on, so he would continue with your normal payments and give you a place to live. I'd say he was more than generous."

Eric sank heavily into the chair and resting his elbows on his knees and his head in his hands. "What am I going to do? The stipend is not enough."

"Unlike you, Eric," said Mellisande. "I won't throw you out, but I do request you move to your apartment as soon as possible."

He quickly lifted his head, his thoughts racing. "What about Helena? When will she be coming home?" Helena needed to die in a tragic accident. Then Mellisande. After that he would be the only one left to inherit.

Mellisande's brows furrowed. "Helena has gone missing. Her father told her he had a man for her to marry and she balked."

"Do you have someone searching?"

"Of course," snapped Mellisande. "Do you think I would leave my child alone to face the dangers of the world? She's been sheltered her entire life. I could not leave her alone now."

"Good. Good. Let me know when you find where she's gone."

"Why would I let you know? You've never cared for Helena. She told me how you treated her in school and she didn't know anything about her father then. Unlike you, who was well aware from the age of eight that Robert was her father." Mellisande narrowed her eyes. "Yet, you kept the secret all these years. I wonder why? What had you expected in return? Hmm?"

Eric had to get to Helena before Mellisande. "I was only mean to her, because I liked her. You know how little boys are."

Mellisande looked him up and down, her gaze raking him. "But you never grew out of it. You were always mean to her. Helena's whereabouts are none of your business."

"I understand your feelings but I, like you, only want to know she is safe."

She cocked an eyebrow and left the room.

Yes, I want to know she's safe. Safely dead.

CHAPTER THREE

April 16, 1887

John and Lena were on the road all day, traveling toward Homestead Canyon. Just after dark they reached a wayfarer's cabin and stopped.

Inside, Lena saw a small fireplace, two sets of narrow bunk beds with ropes, a wooden table with four mismatched chairs and a pot-bellied stove with a coffeepot on the top. She'd never been anywhere so rustic. This would be an adventure. She kept telling herself this was an adventure, and life would be more normal when they reached Homestead Canyon.

"We need our own bedrolls in these cabins. I'll collect the blankets from the wagon. If you want to start the fire, you'll find kindling and wood there on the left side of the fireplace." He pointed at the stacks of fire-building materials. "I'll go fill the bucket with water. There is a creek out back."

"That sounds wonderful. Anything to be off that bench." She rubbed her numb bottom.

"I should have thought of that. You're not used to the buckboard. We'll put a folded blanket under you tomorrow."

"I'll be fine. No need—"

"Tomorrow will be an even longer day than today. You'll appreciate the blanket, believe me."

"All right. If you say so."

After several attempts and many matches, Lena got the fire started in the stove and put the coffee grounds into the pot.

John returned with a metal bucket full of water.

"You can heat this in the fire there's not enough room on the stove top. Then you'll have some water to clean up with." He filled the coffee pot and then set the bucket in the fireplace next to the right wall.

"Thank you. That's very thoughtful."

John smiled.

She liked his smile. He had even white teeth and his blue eyes twinkled.

"So neither of us has to climb into the top bunk, we'll sleep across the room from each other tonight."

He walked up to her and lifted her chin with his finger until she looked at him.

"I can assure you when we get home, we will not be sleeping anywhere but together."

Lena nodded, her cheeks so hot, she was surprised he didn't feel the heat radiating from her. "As I would expect. We are married now, after all."

"We are."

John lowered his head and slanted his lips over hers. He pressed his tongue against her lips.

She gasped, grabbed his shirt and held on.

He took advantage and his tongue forged ahead into her mouth, learned her, dueled with her.

When they broke apart, both were breathless.

"I wish we were home." John rested his chin on the top of her head.

"So do I," Lena said softly.

John pulled her tighter.

"Do you know what you're saying?"

"I think I do. My mother was sure I would know what happened on my wedding night. I'm ready." She looked up at him and smiled. "Are you?" she teased.

John chuckled. "Oh, yes. I'm ready. I've been ready and dreaming about making love to you since I first saw you in the Ritter's living room, your pale blonde hair coming loose from your bun and forming tendrils around your beautiful face. I'd better get the food Mrs. Ritter prepared before I forget myself."

They parted, and John left to bring in the food and place settings for each of them. Just a plate, fork and cup, but that was all they needed for their dinner. Mrs. Ritter had packed fried chicken, potato salad, roast beef sandwiches, cheese, four apples, two pieces of peach pie and two loaves of bread. She also included butter in a small crock and a jar of jelly made from a dark fruit. Perhaps blueberry? She'd find out soon enough, Mrs. Ritter hadn't wanted them to go hungry that was for sure.

Lena poured them each a cup of the strong, hot coffee. She hoped the hot liquid would help her to warm up. She still hadn't taken off her coat, though the fire had heated the room. They sat at the small table and ate in silence.

John was the first to speak. "You came from New Orleans, but I don't detect an accent. You must have lived away from there for a long time."

"I think I told you in my letter about living in a boarding school since I was six. I graduated from the school when I was eighteen and then stayed on as a teacher until just a few months ago. The Oakbridge School is in Connecticut, which is why I don't have an accent. I only left there in September. Then I went to my mother's home where I decided to become a mail-order bride. What about you? Why did you settle in Home-stead Canyon?"

John put down his fork and took a sip of coffee before answering.

"I've traveled about for a long time, working as a farrier."

"What is a farrier?"

"Someone who shoes horses."

"Oh." She forked another bite of the potato salad into her mouth.

"I got tired of the traveling, and when I heard about

the copper strike at Homestead Canyon, I decided it would be as good a place as any to set up a blacksmith shop."

"What's the difference between a blacksmith and a farrier?" The school had horses and there was a blacksmith nearby in the town of Oakbridge. She remembered the sound of the hammer when she'd taken walks on that side of the lake on the school property.

"A blacksmith can do more. I fix wagons, make tools, shoe horses, just about anything you can do with metal, I can do."

John talked with his hands. They waved and emphasized his words.

Lena could tell he was happy to do what he did for a living.

He rested his elbows on the table and held his coffee cup. "What about teaching? What did you teach? Why did you stop?"

"I taught everything from math, to reading, to history. Then I decided I wanted a family… a husband and children of my own. When I was with my mother, I found out a father who I never knew had chosen a husband for me. I immediately refused." That situation still irritated her and it was hard to keep the edge out of her voice. "I wanted to choose my own husband."

"So you went from being given to an unknown man to marrying one."

"You sound just like Mrs. Black at Matchmaker & Co. The answer is no." She reached across the table and placed her hand on his. "I *chose* you. She had other candidates to choose from. I chose you."

He raised an eyebrow and cocked his head. "Why?"

Lena pulled back her hand, took a sip of her still hot coffee and swallowed. "You have kind eyes. Even in the photograph I could see kindness in your eyes." She paused wondering if she should be honest, then deciding it was best if she told him the truth, at least part of it. "And... you were the farthest away from New Orleans."

John laughed and put down his fork. "Ah, now the truth comes out. It's probably time we went to sleep. I want to get an early start tomorrow."

"Yes, I'm tired. Today has been long between the train ride, the wedding and travel here." She stifled a yawn. "I'm actually exhausted."

"Then let's go to sleep. You go on to bed." He pointed at the table. "I'll take care of the dishes."

"That's very nice of you. Thank you."

"You're welcome."

John gathered the dirty plates and found a basin on the shelves next to the stove. Cobwebs and dirt were inside, but he brushed them out and used it for washing. The bucket of warm water he used to rinse. After he was done, he took the bucket outside. He was gone for a few minutes and then came back with another bucket full of water.

Lena watched him as he did the dishes knowing this was a chore that would soon be hers.

He placed the bucket in the fire that was mostly coals and added a couple pieces of wood until the fire danced merrily. "It'll still be warm by tomorrow morning."

"Thank you. I appreciate it."

Lena turned down the blankets on her bed. She had two blankets each folded in half. With the equivalent of four blankets on top of her and still wearing her coat surely she would finally get warm. Still wearing her corset, she knew sleep would be difficult to come by, but exhaustion claimed her.

She lay down on the mattress and pulled the blankets over her. Slowly, warmth seeped into her body and her eyelids closed.

"Good night, John," she said before sleep overtook her.

"Good night, Lena."

Lena awoke feeling deliciously warm. She was loath to get out of the cocoon she'd made.

"Up and at 'em," said John. "I know you're awake. We've got to eat and get going if we're to reach home before dark."

She threw back the blankets and was immediately hit by cold air. The fire was burning brightly but hadn't yet taken the chill off the room. She rubbed her arms vigorously hoping to warm up.

"The water is heated if you want to wash."

"I do. Thank you. I need to get the sleep off my face and wake up." John had put a washcloth and towel on the table next to what was left of their food. They'd finished the chicken last night, but roast beef sandwiches, potato salad and apple pie remained for breakfast. They would eat the cheese, apples, and bread at midday. The food was enough to sustain them until they reached home and she could make something for dinner.

After eating and washing the dishes, John used the dirty water to douse the fire. Then he made sure to provide a supply of kindling and firewood for the next traveler.

True to his word, John folded one of the blankets so it acted as a cushion on the wagon seat.

Lena was more than grateful. Her behind was tender from the train and the buckboard so the cushioning was very welcome.

"Tell me about Homestead Canyon."

"The town is very small. I hope you don't mind small towns... *very* small towns. Hanover is a city compared to Homestead Canyon."

"Oh, my." She wasn't sure how she felt about that, other than she would be harder to find, and that was a good thing.

"The town is growing. Miners are coming every day and several new businesses are opening, too."

"That's wonderful. Do many women live there?"

"A few. There is Mrs. Cornelia Goode. You can go to her if you have any question about anything. She's lived there the longest. Then there's Lola Kerr, she's the second person I'd ask. Rosalind Van Dyke is fairly new. She's married to the mayor and mine owner, Peter

Van Dyke and has been there less than a year. Then there are two saloon girls, Ruby and Jolene. Others live there but those are the ones I think of off the top of my head."

"I hope I can make friends with them." Lena hadn't had many friends. When she had arrived at The Oakbridge School, she'd spoken with a New Orleans accent. Teased unmercifully by the other students, she quickly learned to speak without it. After that, she'd tended to keep to herself for fear someone would find out about her mother, or that she had no father.

Yet she'd always wanted to be like the other children and go home on holidays. That wasn't ever possible. First, because New Orleans was so far away and second, her mother's business didn't accommodate the needs of children.

She didn't like to think about her childhood. All she was sure of was her children would never have to go through what she did. She was married and they would have a father.

They'd been on the road all day and had just crested a hill when buildings came into view. The setting sun forced her to shade her eyes. She pointed toward the few buildings she could see and hoped there was part of the town she couldn't see. "Look! Is that Homestead Canyon?"

"Yes. We live on the far side of town. We'll be home soon, but we still have a few miles to go."

About a half hour later, John pulled in front of a small cabin.

Not exactly the house Lena had been hoping for, but it didn't matter. It was her home.

"I know it's not big." He set the brake. "But we can add on to it as much as you want."

He jumped down and came around to her side and lifted her to the ground.

"It's wonderful." Her heart soared. It could be a castle and she wouldn't love it more. "It's ours. No one can take it away from me. This is *my* home."

If John thought anything about her declaration he didn't say, but he did have a wide smile on his face.

When they got to the front door, John opened it, then picked Lena up and carried her across the threshold.

They were in the main room of the cabin that served as the kitchen, dining and living rooms combined. A door on the wall next to the fireplace led to the bedroom. The fireplace was built so that it heated both the main room and the bedroom so she saw through the space and made out the bed against the far wall. Lena shivered. The house had been closed for four days and was cold inside.

"I'll get a fire started and it won't take long for it to heat up in here."

Soon John had a roaring fire going.

Lena stood in front of the blaze, turning so her front warmed, then her back and then her front again. She repeated the motion until she finally was warm and took off her coat.

John brought in her trunks and valise, putting them in the living room.

"Not enough room in the bedroom."

"That's all right. It will be easier to empty them in here, anyway. Not all the contents are clothes."

"There's a closet in the bedroom." He grinned. "Let me show you."

She raised an eyebrow. "All right." What could be so special about a closet? The cabin was rustic, but she loved it. She'd never lived anyplace like it before and yet she felt more comfortable here than in her mother's lavish mansion.

He took her by the hand and pulled her into the bedroom.

The room was actually very large, almost as big as the living room, kitchen and dining room together. The centerpiece was the bed. Lena had never seen such a big bed in her life. To the right of the bed was a wooden nightstand and on the next wall a bureau and a door, presumably to the closet. To the left of the bed was the second nightstand, and on the wall to her left sat a tallboy dresser made of dark word that matched the rest of the furniture and commode.

John took her to the closet door.

"Go ahead and look. I designed this cabin with a wife in mind, even though it's small."

She opened the door and her mouth dropped open. A window in the far wall allowed her to see the hanging clothes. Under the window stood a short, three-drawer wooden dresser and rods hung on the other two sides of the room.

"John. It's wonderful. This is a lovely home. It's as

though you built it with me in mind, not just any woman."

She stood on tiptoe and kissed his cheek, the bristle of his beard tickled her lips.

"Oh, no." He wrapped an arm around her waist and pulled her against him. "When we're together, just the two of us, I plan on really kissing you. Like this."

His mouth covered hers and he gave her another of his earth-shattering kisses. Kisses that curled her toes and made her tingle all over. Then he leaned back and grinned.

"Oh, my." She touched her lips sure they were swollen.

"Now, I'll take care of the horses and the wagon, I also have to check on the cow and the other two horses, Star and Jasper. There is food in the cupboards and eggs, meat and milk in the icebox. Make sure it's not spoiled. If you would prepare dinner, please, I'd appreciate it very much. Lunch was too long ago and I'm starving. I bet you're hungry, too."

"I am. I'll see what you have and get something cooking."

She followed him out of the bedroom and went to the kitchen. It wasn't a bad space at all. Along the side wall was a long counter with a dry sink and many drawers, large and small, underneath. On the right side of the sink stood an icebox. On the same wall as the fireplace sat a four-burner, wood-burning stove with piles of wood and kindling next to it. Across the room from the stove were shelves holding all sorts of food stuffs… canned goods, as well as dry staples.

Lena looked in the icebox and found it full. Two dozen eggs, milk, three pounds of bacon and a large roast that she assumed was beef, but could have been elk or deer. A couple of steaks and two chickens ready for frying filled out the rest of the icebox. She sniffed the milk and it still smelled sweet. There was a breadbox on the counter with bread in it. She decided to make them breakfast as that was quick and easy. She also didn't have to figure out a recipe. She'd cook the roast, whatever it was, for dinner tomorrow.

By the time John finished putting away the animals, making sure all his horses and the cow were also fed and watered, breakfast was ready. She'd scrambled eight eggs, fried one of the full pounds of bacon and toasted six slices of bread in a second skillet. That should hold John for a while. She would have to learn how much food he ate and prepare enough, but that knowledge would come with time.

After they ate, Lena stood to clear the table and wash the dishes, but John grabbed her hand.

"I've waited as long as I can. I want to make love to you Lena and seal our wedding vows."

She lowered her gaze to the wood slat floor and felt heat invade her cheeks.

"I'm not sure, John. We don't know each other and though we need to make love to consummate the marriage, I'd prefer to wait for a while. Until we really know each other."

He pulled her into his arms, "There's no better way to get to know someone than by making love to them."

"No. I don't think so."

"I thought you said your mother had prepared you for your wedding night?"

"She did but…"

"But what?"

She glanced away. "You're so big," she whispered.

He chuckled. "Very well. I know that you're untried, and so we'll postpone this until you aren't so frightened. I assure you nothing about the act of making love should scare you. I'm big that's true, but I assure you Lena, you and I will be perfect together."

Shaking her head, she murmured, "I don't think so. I need to know you more than just a day or two. Please, John."

"I'll not take you against your will. But one day, you and I will make love, and you'll be glad we did. In the meantime, you'll sleep with me and get used to my body. Once you get comfortable, we'll move on. I won't wait forever, Lena."

She nodded, knowing if he wanted to, he could force her, and she could do nothing. It was his right to claim her as his wife, body and soul.

That night Lena readied herself for bed. The weather was still cold and although the house was warm now, by morning there would be a chill again just as there had been at the school in Connecticut. In Denver, she'd purchased several styles of nightgowns, from flannel to the lightest silk. Tonight was definitely a night for flannel.

She dropped the nightgown over her head and put on the matching dressing gown before joining John in the living room.

He sat in one of the rocking chairs, whittling wood, the shavings going into a bucket so he didn't make a mess.

"Do you mind if I read for a while?"

"Not at all. Why don't you read out loud? I always enjoy a good story."

Lena smiled. "You sound like my students. They always wanted me to read to them."

"You have a beautiful voice. You know it's all an excuse to hear your voice."

She laughed. "I'll remember that and one of these days I'll have you read."

"Oww. Dang it."

"What happened?" She looked down at his hands and saw one of them was bleeding. "You've cut your-self. You're as bad as some of my students. Come with me."

Lena walked to the kitchen, John followed in her wake.

"I'll get some water so we can clean the wound."

"It's nothing, Lena. Really."

"Nonsense. You've got to clean the cut or it could become infected. You don't want that."

"No, I don't suppose I do."

She looked up and saw John staring with a smile on his face.

"What?" she asked.

"Having someone take care of me is nice."

"Wives… and husbands… take care of each other. It's what married people do."

"I haven't had anyone take care of me since I was ten years old."

"What happened then?"

John's features clouded over.

"My mother died."

"Oh, John. I'm so sorry."

Immediately she realized she was lucky in some ways that she still had her mother even if she could never introduce her to John. He wouldn't understand. He would think that she was like her mother and she wasn't. She was the opposite of her mother. But what if he found out?

She dipped hot water into a basin from the bucket on the stove and added cold water from the bucket on the counter. "Here wash your hands in the basin."

Lena gathered bandages from the shelf in the kitchen where she'd spotted them.

"Dry your hands."

She handed him a towel.

"Now, let's see what we have here."

She held his hand and examined the cut, then looked upward. "It's not too bad but I'll put on a bandage to keep it clean." Lena tore a strip of cloth about two inches wide from the larger piece. Then she wrapped

John's finger. When she finished, she tore the strip down the middle for about three inches before wrapping one side under his finger and tying the two ends together.

"That should hold for a while. Now why don't you quit whittling, while I read *Moby Dick* by Herman Melville. You haven't read it before, have you?"

"No, can't say that I have."

"Oh good. It's my first time, too. I'll start at the beginning."

They retreated to the living room and sat in the rockers there. Lena opened the book and began to read. *"Call me Ishmael."*

She read for an hour, until her voice was tired. "Time for bed. I can't read any more tonight."

Resting his elbows on the chair arms, he leaned back as she finished. "Now I know why your students wanted you to read to them. You bring the story to life, with your different voices for the characters. The result is like watching a play, not just listening to a book being read."

She dipped her head. "Thank you. That's very kind of you to say."

"Nothing kind about it. It's the truth. But enough of this. I'm ready to have you in my arms."

Her head snapped up, her pulse quickened and her stomach suddenly fluttered. "What?"

"I'm holding you tonight, Lena. I can't make love to you, and I won't until you say so, but I still want to hold you, feel your body next to mine."

"I... I..."

John reached over and stroked a knuckle down her

cheek. "I don't want you to fear me. This way we'll get used to each other and when the time comes, you won't be afraid."

---

*T*he third morning of their marriage, John woke her before the sun came up.

"Get up, sleepyhead. Time to milk the cow. I've had Lester Goode doing the milking for me while I was gone, but now that we're back, we need to do the job."

"What?" she said sleepily and turned her back to him.

He grabbed the blankets and pulled them off her onto the floor.

"Let's go. Get up and get dressed."

She opened one eye and glared at him. What did she know of milking a cow? The school had cows, but she didn't know how to milk one.

"All right. Give me a few minutes, please."

"I'll get coffee started. By the time you're done with the cow, the coffee will be brewed and then you can start breakfast."

He left her lying on the bed. She had to either get up or freeze to death. Rising she walked to the bureau with the pitcher and basin. Taking a washcloth from the small stack next to the basin, she poured water on it and bracing herself, washed her face. The cold water awakened her like nothing else could.

She donned her most serviceable dress—a plain

brown cotton with gathering over the bustle and lace at the cuff and neckline. Last, she put her hair into a loose bun at the nape of her neck. Checking her reflection in the mirror and finding it pleasing enough, she walked into the kitchen.

John waited at the table for her.

She saw the large coffeepot on the stove. He'd started the fire in the fireplace, too. When they came back inside, they'd enter a warm house.

"I'm ready."

"It's cold outside. Best you put on your coat."

She nodded, pulled the outer garment off the peg next to the front door and slipped her arms into it. Then she put on her hat and gloves, too.

"You won't be able to keep the gloves on. It's much easier to milk her when you can feel her teat."

"Well, I'm sure she'll appreciate my having warm hands to milk her with."

John smiled. "You might be right about that."

They walked out to the little barn where he kept his twohorses and the cow. After entering, John grabbed a small stool and a bucket from a place on the floor by the cow's stall.

"This is Marybelle. She's a good cow." He patted her on the rump. "Aren't you, Marybelle?"

He set the stool next to the animal and the bucket underneath her udder. Then he pushed the full udder around with his hands like he was loosening up everything inside it.

Next he took a teat in each hand and pulled,

squeezed and pulled again and again until the milk began to flow. The first few squirts landed on the ground, and suddenly three cats were there to lap up the milk that hit the floor. Then he moved the direction of the teat toward the bucket and started squeezing them alternating the squeezes with each hand.

The milk flowed easily, and he squeezed until the bucket was about half full.

"Now it's your turn."

He stood and relinquished the stool to her.

Lena sat, stretching to reach the teats and discovered she needed to move the stool closer. Her arms and legs were so much shorter than John's.

Once she got settled on the stool, she grabbed the teats and pulled. Nothing happened. She looked up at John.

"Go ahead and try again. This time squeeze and pull." He showed her with his hands. "Squeeze and pull."

She nodded, did exactly as he said and forced a dribble from each teat. Disappointed and determined, she repeated the process again and again, until she finally got a good squirt... that landed milk all over John's boot.

"Oh, I'm so sorry."

"Don't be. Go on ahead and pull some more."

She did and low and behold the milk started to flow. Pleased with herself, Lena kept it up until the bucket was nearly full and the udder stopped giving milk.

"Congratulations on milking your first cow."

Lena, quite proud of herself, grinned up at him. "I really did it. I milked a cow."

"Yup and you'll be milking her from now on."

"Surely, we don't have to get up so early every morning, do we?"

"Afraid we do. Need to milk the cow and feed the chickens before breakfast. In case you're wondering what I'm doing, I feed the animals and take care of anything else that needs doing in the mornings. Like when it snows, I'm the one who shovels the path to the barn."

Lena sighed. "All right. What do I do with this milk?"

"Take it to the house and strain it through cheese-cloth into another bucket. You'll find it in the second drawer to the left of the sink. Then put it in the icebox. The milk from yesterday will go to the store to sell."

Lena stood and stretched, placing her hands on the small of her back and bending backwards. "Why not just take the fresh milk to the store? The milk in the icebox is good and cold and ready for use. We can use it until it's gone and then start over."

"No one wants to buy warm milk. That's why yesterday's milk goes to the store."

"You're right. I understand now. What would you like for breakfast?" Add this to the list of things she had to remember.

John picked up the milking stool and put it back just outside the cow's stall. "A repeat of last night's dinner would be great, with some bread and butter. There's also service berry jam in the icebox."

"What are service berries?"

"They're like a wild plum. Very sweet and tasty."

"Hmm. That's interesting. Maybe Mrs. Goode can show me so I can pick them."

"I'm sure she can since she's the one who gave me the jelly."

Lena smiled. "Yes, I guess she could. Now, how many eggs?"

"Ten ought to do it and whatever you want."

Lena's eyes got wide. "Ten eggs? Should I cook a whole pound of bacon, too?"

"That would be great. I can take a bacon sandwich for a snack."

"Where is your blacksmith shop? Is it close enough for you to be home for lunch or should I figure out something for you to take along?"

"The shop is by the mine a couple of miles from here. I can come home for lunch because I ride my horse, Jasper. There's a couple of steaks in the icebox you can fry up for lunch and you'll find a jar of green beans and potatoes on the shelf that Cornelia Goode gave me."

"And what about dinner?"

Lena was beginning to think her entire day would consist of preparing food for her large husband. She realized he was a big man and he did work hard, so she didn't resent the cooking, just wondered when she'd have time to do anything else.

"An elk roast and a couple of chickens ready for frying are in the icebox."

"Yes, I saw them. Do you mind if I cut up the roast and fry it? One of the women at the school taught me to fry venison in strips to make it more tender, and it occurs to me that same thing can be done with elk."

"You can do what you want. Cooking is not my specialty. You might want to do what is easiest until you settle into your work schedule. I'll take care of feeding the horses and the cow before I come back to the house."

"All right. I'll see you then."

Lena carried the fresh milk to the house and strained it through the cheesecloth to remove any particulate matter that might have dropped inside. Then she set the bucket of fresh liquid aside while she cooked breakfast.

After breakfast, John came back into the kitchen. "It's still early. Would you like to see the town?"

"Yes, I'd like that very much." She dried her hands on a towel and set it on the counter next to the sink. "Won't the walk take time from your work?"

"No one is going to get anything until I arrive. I'm my own boss, so I set my own hours."

"Oh, good. Let me get my coat."

Retrieving her garment from a peg by the door, she pulled her hat and gloves out of the pockets, and slipped them on, before donning the coat.

"Don't you have a hat and gloves? How do you stay warm?"

He laughed. "The weather is not that cold. You're

just used to the temperature in New Orleans. It's much, much warmer there."

"Hmpft. I'd only been in New Orleans for about six months. Before that I was in Connecticut and they have very cold winters. I'm used to bundling up to go outside in the winter." She buttoned up and was especially glad she'd spent the extra money for a heavy wool coat rather than the lighter weight ones that were available. "All right. I'm ready."

He held the door open then followed her out. Once on the road he held out his arm toward her.

She put both of her hands around his arm and they walked the ten minutes to town.

"There is not too much to see." John pointed at a gray house with white trim and a white porch. "That house belongs to the mayor and his wife, Peter and Rosalind Van Dyke. He also owns the land the town sits on, the boarding house, the store and, of course, the mine."

Lena thought the house was quite pretty and the white trim perfect against the dark gray. She was amazed by the new, yet beautiful landscape. Scrub oak and pine trees dotted an otherwise vacant landscape. Everything was covered with snow or mud. The road was mud from the horses and wagons that constantly drove up and down from the mine.

Farther on, he pointed out the boarding house, a two-story clapboard building which appeared to have a new coat of white paint. A long inviting porch ran the front of the building, with welcoming benches on either side of the door. The store was a one-story building with two gleaming front windows. There was no name on the building, just *Store*.

Finally they passed the saloon, a two-story clapboard building also painted white with a large sign on the front of the second story saying *SALOON*. Past the saloon were cabins and beyond that were tents with, unless her nose betrayed her, pig pens behind them.

"Homestead Canyon is a real small place, but it's a good place full of good people."

She squeezed his arm. "I don't mind a little town. I grew up in large cities and I prefer Homestead Canyon." She would have to make some adjustments, like planning meals for a week and getting those foods all at once. There was no running to the store to get something because the store may not have what she might need.

"Hello, John." A short, round woman with very white hair waved to them as they passed the cabins.

"Hello, Cornelia. How do you fare today?"

She chuckled. "Finer than a frog's hair."

John laughed and nodded.

"I don't understand," *Did I miss something.* Lena cocked her head and looked up at John. "Why is that funny?"

He shook his head. "Because frogs don't have hair and if they do, it's so fine, you can't see it."

Lena smiled and then laughed. "I understand. She was saying she was very good, very fine indeed."

"Exactly."

"Who you got there with you, John?"

Cornelia walked to the edge of the road.

"My wife. Lena Thorpe, meet Cornelia Goode. She's the one I mentioned that you could ask any question of."

Cornelia extended her hand. "That's right, Mrs. Thorpe, Lena if I may. We're not too formal around here."

Lena shook hands with the older woman. "Oh, of course. Call me Lena, please."

"Good. Now John is right. I'll answer any question you might have and if I don't know the answer, I'll find someone who does."

"That's so very kind. I have to admit, I'm not a very good cook." Lena saw John's worried expression and added, "though I can guarantee John won't go hungry."

He smiled.

"I'm not the best either, but I can bake pretty well and Rosalind Van Dyke has a recipe for biscuits that is wonderful."

"I don't bake at all. So on that front I need all the help I can get."

"Come over Saturday morning about ten, and we'll have a little lesson in baking."

"Thank you. I'd love that."

"Lola Kerr and Rosalind will both be there. We're sharing what we know."

"I'll be there. Thank you. It has been very nice meeting you."

"You, too. Guess I better finish my chores." Cornelia nodded at John and turned back to her cabin.

"What a nice lady."

"Yes, she is."

"Will the store have the groceries I need, or should I make a list for your next trip to Hanover?" She turned and gestured toward the store.

"Make a list, but you can give it to the storekeeper, Roscoe Jones, and he'll order it. Sam Bowmen comes through twice a week and brings goods from Hanover."

Lena sighed. How would she ever remember everything to do?

CHAPTER FOUR

hey turned before they reached the tents and walked back toward home. As they passed the mayor's house, they saw a tall woman come out.

She looked up as they passed.

"John. John Thorpe." She waved. "Who is that with you?"

The woman hurried down the steps and out to the street.

She wore a beautiful lavender shirtwaist blouse and matching skirt with a bow that draped over each side of the small bustle. As she got closer Lena saw the woman had a rather plain face, but her smile and the twinkle in her eye made her lovely.

"Ah, Mrs. Van Dyke, may I present my wife Lena. We just arrived home last night."

"What have I told you, John? I'm Rosalind."

She came forward and took Lena's free hand in both of hers.

"I'm so happy to meet you. It's wonderful to have another woman here. I hope you'll find our little town to your liking. Where are you from, my dear?"

"New Orleans, ma'am, but I spent most of my life in Connecticut."

"Oh, New Orleans." Rosalind raised her chin a bit and looked toward the sky. "I always wanted to go there. Perhaps I can convince Peter to take me once the baby comes." She looked down and placed both hands on her growing stomach.

"Congratulations. When is the baby due?" asked Lena.

"July."

"Oh, how wonderful. A baby to celebrate Independence Day, perhaps?"

"Yes, perhaps. Peter and I are very happy."

"Well, we must be on our way," said John. "Good to see you Mrs.... Rosalind. And congratulations."

"Yes, very nice to meet you. If a visit to New Orleans is planned, I can tell you some places to see and you really should stay at the Hotel Monteleone. It was built just last year and is quite lovely. I'm sure you would enjoy your stay there." Lena put her hand back through the crook of John's elbow. "I hope we'll see each other often."

"Thank you for the recommendation. And you can count on seeing more of me," said Rosalind with a smile. "With so few of us ladies, we have to stick together."

Would Lena soon be in the family way? She hoped

so. She wanted a child of her own very much, but that would mean making love with John. Lena wasn't sure she was ready for that part of their relationship just yet, regardless of her bravado when they had been in the wayfarers' cabin.

That evening after dinner, Lena looked in her trunk and saw all her books at the bottom. "John, you don't have any bookshelves. Can you build me a couple? Then we can put out our books for easier access."

"I never had need of bookshelves before." He continued working with his knife on a small piece of wood.

She cocked her head. "Maybe if you read, you wouldn't need to whittle so much and save your poor hands a couple of scars. Don't you like to read?"

"No… I…" He set aside his project and his expression turned serious. "You might as well know. I can't read. I can write my name and do numbers in my head, but reading was never necessary. My ma and pa couldn't read either."

"Oh, John." You've been deprived of so much wonderful knowledge.

He lowered his head with his hands hanging loose between his knees. "Don't look at me like that. I don't need your pity. I get along just fine."

Lena sat on the floor at his feet and gazed up at him. "There is no reason for you to be ashamed that you did not learn. I'll teach you. No one else has to know."

"Mrs. Van Dyke knows. She helped me write the letters to the matchmaker."

"Then she'll be the only one in Homestead Canyon who will know you couldn't read before now." She chuckled. "I wondered about that. The handwriting was so neat. We'll begin tonight. Put away your whittling, Mr. Thorpe, you're starting school now."

She rose and picked up Moby Dick from the table between the rocking chairs.

"You're enjoying this one so far, I'm sure you'll like the rest of the book. It's an adventure story."

Lena went to the table and John followed her. She pulled her chair next to his at the rectangular table. She got a piece of paper and a pencil from those that John kept to do his numbers.

"First, you're learning the alphabet, then we'll work on sounds. After that I'll make you a primer like I used to teach the students at the school. It won't be easy, but the world will open up to you once you can read."

And so, they began reading together every night. For the next week, John would come home, wash, they would eat a quick supper and then read the primer or work on writing his alphabet and copying the story she was writing for him until bedtime.

Every night she would read to him from *Moby Dick*. She was surprised when he asked her to read a paragraph and then let him see if he could read it back to her. He did remarkably well. So, at the end of each lesson, she would read a couple of paragraphs or a page and then let him read the same back to her.

Lena was amazed at the progress John was making. He loved reading, even when he stumbled on words.

She'd correct him, he'd repeat after her a couple of times, and then that word was one he didn't stumble over again. He was a very quick study, and Lena couldn't have been prouder of him.

Each night she discovered what a gentle man he was, and she found herself falling for her husband. When she thought of him, she had a warmth in her heart she'd never felt before. Lena thought that must be love. The joy of being with him, whether to read or talk. The gentle way he taught her how to feed chickens, and the patience he showed when she learned to milk their cow.

She still chuckled under her breath when she remembered the first time she'd milked the cow and squirted him as he squatted next to her. Those first few times, milk went everywhere until she learned how to hold the teat correctly.

Lena learned what day of the week John was used to having things done. Monday was laundry, Tuesday ironing, Wednesday she did her baking for the week ahead. Thursday, she dusted. Friday, she washed the windows inside and if the weather was nice outside too. She swept the floors and made the bed every day.

On Saturdays Lena went to Mrs. Goode's and learned to bake. She brought home the cakes and pies that John loved. One special Saturday, Mrs. Van Dyke taught them all how to make her special biscuits. Her secret ingredient, she said to the group, was love. Lena agreed. Everything she cooked and everything she baked for John was full of love.

Baths were taken once per week, much to her regret,

on Saturday nights. She took spit baths every day and would have liked to have had a real bath instead, but she understood. Heating the water on the stove in buckets, hauling the long metal tub in and out of the house, made taking a bath more like work than the relaxing activity she was used to.

Sundays were just like any other day unless the Reverend and Mrs. Ritter came to town. He tried to come every couple of months but with his own flock to care for in Hanover he couldn't come more often. So, on most Sunday's they used the time for extra reading lessons or simply to talk about their lives together. This was one of the more difficult days, because she couldn't talk about Mellisande or what she did for a living.

Luckily, since John started learning to read, every precious moment that he could get was spent reading and learning to write as well. Lena didn't have to tell him about Mellisande. The longer she could put that off, the better. She wanted John to be in love with her before he found out about her mother.

She'd been in Homestead Canyon for two weeks now and John was ever patient with her. He held her at night and didn't insist that they make love, for which she was grateful. She remembered the first morning she'd woken up next to him, she'd been so embarrassed and more than a little surprised that her arm was thrown across him.

She'd opened her eyes to a magnificent feeling of warmth. Lena moved away from where she had cuddled into his side and removed her arm from him, trying to be careful and not wake him.

"You're awake, I see."

She stilled and closed her eyes.

He chuckled. "I'm still here. Closing your eyes won't make me go away,"

She sighed and moved out of his embrace making sure her nightgown covered everything before she got out of the bed.

He let her go.

"I was hoping you weren't awake, and I could escape without waking you."

"Escape? I'm your husband. You have no need to escape me."

"I just meant that I wouldn't be embarrassed by you knowing that I cuddled with you."

"You did that almost as soon as you fell asleep. You moved to the warmth. Considering as cold as you've been, you should feel much better today."

She nodded. "I do. It's the first time I've been warm in the last week. Since before I left Golden, Colorado and Mrs. Black's office. Come to think about it, I haven't been warm since I left New Orleans, which is very odd because I grew up in Connecticut and they have cold winters, too. I guess six months in New Orleans was enough for me to get acclimated to the warm weather."

He put his arms behind his head.

The blankets rode uncomfortably low on his body for her peace of mind. He was a beautiful man. His arms were heavily muscled and with his broad chest and flat stomach, he was simply a treat to look at. She couldn't believe this handsome man was hers. Her husband. And he was kind on top of that. What had she done to deserve this gift?

John threw back the blankets and swung his legs over the side of the bed.

"Oh, my," Lena squeezed her eyes shut at the same moment she heard his chuckle.

"You can look now."

He'd donned his pants. Pulling his socks out of his boots and grabbing a shirt from the closet he finished dressing.

Now two weeks later, she was used to sleeping beside him. No surprises happened when she awoke because she knew she'd have her arm across him come morning.

After her first request, John hung a rope across one corner of the room. Lena secured a blanket to the line with clothespins and used this space for dressing and to hold the chamber pot.

John wasn't particularly happy about the curtain, but he only complained once. "I like to watch you undress," he'd said.

"I don't like being watched. That may change some-day, but today is not that day."

*M*ay 16, 1887

*J*ohn struggled to believe he and Lena had been married for more than a month. He chuckled when he remembered Lena's comment from that morning. She was right today might not be the day she'd let him make love to her or watch her undress, but she was coming around to the idea. She was becoming accustomed to him.

She was a patient teacher, and he supposed he could be patient, too. The last thing in the world he wanted was to scare her. She was so tiny. A good foot shorter than he, she was a sprite to his giant.

He didn't blame her for wanting to take having relations slow. She was a virgin and of good morals. That's what he asked for and he could tell by what he'd come to know of Lena, that she was both of those things.

Perhaps he'd try to woo her. Just because they were married didn't mean she didn't want to be courted. He'd talk to Rosalind. She'd know what he needed to do to court his wife because Rosalind was a lady and came from the big city of St. Louis.

He walked into town, to the Van Dyke residence and knocked on the heavy wooden door.

Lola Kerr answered.

"Good afternoon, John."

"Good afternoon, Lola. Is Rosalind in?"

"Yes. Come in. Come in."

Lola stepped back and held the door open for him to pass.

"She's in the study. Follow me."

"That's all right. I know the way."

Lola nodded and headed in the direction of the kitchen.

John went to the left and found the study door wide open. He knocked.

Rosalind looked up from her papers.

"Why, John, good afternoon. What can I do for you today? Do you have a note you'd like to have written? Come. Sit."

John entered the room and sat in the sturdy leather chair in front of the desk. "No, I told Lena I couldn't read or write and she's teaching me. What I need from you today is to know how to court my wife. We're married and all, but I think Lena… that she… well that she needs to be courted and made to feel special." *Then maybe she'll consider making love more favorably.*

"That's wonderful. I sometimes wish Peter had courted me. But in any case, you should bring her presents, just little things like flowers, although this is not the time of year for them. Down at the store we have some ribbon and stick candy, hard candy like hore-hound, maybe a new book. You know we take orders all the time, so if you want something special we'll order it for you."

"I'll go down to the store and see what they have." John stood. "Thank you, Mrs. … er… Rosalind."

"You're welcome. Anytime."

He left and walked directly to the store. The sun was shining bright, just like his mood. Somehow, he was certain courting Lena was the right thing to do.

"Hi, Roscoe."

"John." Roscoe nodded his balding head ever so slightly. "What can I do for you today?"

"I'm looking for some gewgaws for Mrs. Thorpe."

"There are ribbons and combs and such there under the side window."

John strode over and looked at the female things the store carried. Which of these things would Lena like? She already had a lot of this kind of stuff, so he decided on candy.

On the counter stood ten glass jars with sticks of hard candy inside—so many flavors. The candy was a penny a stick. John picked out two sticks each of five different kinds. He chose lemon, orange, cherry, honey and of course, peppermint. Maybe Lena would share with him.

He handed Roscoe the candy and a dime.

Roscoe placed the candy in a paper bag and handed it to John.

"Thanks, Roscoe. I'm sure the missus will enjoy these."

"Hey, Sam was in with the mail today. There's a letter here for your wife, if she's Hellna DuBoys."

Roscoe hadn't said the names correctly, but John knew about whom he spoke.

"Yes, that's her. Who's the letter from?"

"It says Simon and Goldstein, Attorneys at Law."

He looked up with a wide smile, clearly happy he could read the letter.

John was jealous of Roscoe for that knowledge.

"They's, in New York City. Looks like they is some kinda high fallutin lawyers. Is Lena in some kind of trouble?"

John shook his head. "None that we know about." He held his hand out for the letter.

Roscoe placed it in his hand and then stood there, waiting.

"Ain't you gonna open it?"

"The letter's for Lena not me." He didn't want Roscoe to know that he couldn't read the letter if he'd wanted to.

"But she's yer wife. You kin open her mail 'cause anything she has belongs to you."

John rolled his eyes. "Spoken like a true unmarried man."

He slipped the letter and the candy bag into the inside pocket of his coat.

What would a New York lawyer want with Lena?

CHAPTER FIVE

*L*ena saw Matt walking past the house and ran outside. She recognized the child from John's description. He was so cute with his bright, curly red hair and freckles.

"Young man, young man."

He walked over to her.

"You're Matt, aren't you? I'm Lena. John's wife."

"Yes'um, I'm Matt."

"I'm new in town and you know everyone, so I wondered if you would know who would want to read my magazine now that I'm done with it? I'd hate to just throw it away when someone else could enjoy it. Maybe you could give it to someone for me, please?"

She handed Matt her copy of Harpers Bazaar that she'd carried from Denver. Lena was surprised a month had passed before she'd finished reading the magazine.

"Oh, yes, ma'am, I'm sure I can find someone who would want to read it."

"Thank you so much. You have a good day now."

"Oh, I will Miz Thorpe. Thank you, ma'am. You have a good day, too."

Lena watched the boy scamper away, the magazine clutched in his hand.

*D*uring the walk home, John found the letter addressed to Helena foremost on his mind. What would lawyers in New York want with Lena?

When he arrived at his house, he went inside and didn't see her so he looked in the bedroom. No Lena. What was today? Ah, wash day. She should be outside.

John walked out the kitchen door that led directly to the backyard and the clothesline. There he found Lena standing on a chair and pinning his clothes to dry. They'd had snow a couple of days ago and patches of white ice still remained.

Anxiety gripped him and he ran to her.

"What are you doing up there? You could fall and break your neck. You've got the chair sitting on ice."

She looked toward the ground. "I hadn't noticed. How else am I to reach this line?"

Lena climbed down, moved the chair, grabbed the last piece of the clothing, positioned the chair and climbed back up to hang the blouse.

"Here." He grabbed the garment from her and helped her down from the chair. "Let me." John pinned the blouse to the line.

She picked up the chair in one hand and the basket in the other.

"Let me take those, too."

John reached out and relieved Lena of the items.

"Thank you. That's very nice."

"I'm going to ask Mrs. Kerr to take care of our laundry."

"That's not necessary." She opened the door to the kitchen. "I'm managing just fine."

He put the basket on the porch and followed her inside with the chair. "Lena, it's time we had a talk."

She stilled, knowing what he was going to say. Was she ready? Yes, she'd been here nearly five weeks and yes, she was ready for her husband to make love to her.

"I agree we need to talk."

"Ladies, first."

She turned her back and went to the kitchen sink and gazed out the window.

"I'm ready to truly become your wife, but only if you still want me."

Silence.

She turned.

John grinned. Finally, he'd get to make sweet love to his wife. His patience had been worth it.

"I couldn't have said it better, except the part about do I still want you. The answer is more than ever."

He realized he was still holding the chair and set it down at the table. Then he walked up behind her and clasped her upper arms in his hands. While he rubbed up and down her arms, he leaned in and whispered in her ear.

"Are you sure?"

He kissed the sensitive skin beneath her ear.

She shivered.

"J... John."

He turned her in his arms and his lips found hers.

Lena lifted herself to her tiptoes, wrapped her arms around his neck and kissed him back.

John lifted her, put her legs around his waist and walked into the bedroom where he set her softly on the bed.

"I know this is your first time and I will be as gentle as I can be."

"I trust you."

He couldn't have been more pleased with her words. "Good."

*J*ohn was a tender lover and though there had been some pain, she felt wonderful now.

They lay together. Her mind worked too much to rest. What will happen now? Do we just go about our regular day?

"You're thinking too much," grumbled John.

"I'm just wondering what we do now."

"Well, I for one am going back to work, though I'd

like to make love to you again, I know you'll be too sore."

"So we won't do that anymore?" she teased.

John laughed. "Oh, my sweet Lena. We'll be doing that often and with much gusto. I'd like to see you round with my child."

She smiled. "I would like that as well."

She scooted to the side of the bed, threw off the covers and ran for the curtain hanging in the corner.

"Don't you think we could take that down now? I've seen you naked as the day you were born. You don't need to hide any longer."

Lena peeked around the side of the curtain. "Not until you get me a folding screen."

"But like I said—"

"I know what you said, but I like to have some privacy and this arrangement gives me that."

"All right, when I can afford one, I'll get you a screen. Oh, by the way, I picked up the mail when I was out earlier. A letter arrived for you."

Lena became very still a knot forming in her stomach. Who could know she was here?

"Who was the letter addressed to?"

"It's addressed to Helena DuBois." He chuckled. "You should have heard Roscoe when he read that to me. It's from Simon and Goldstein, an attorney in New York City."

Lena came out from behind the curtain.

"You're still naked." His smile faded as he watched

her. "Lena? You're shaking." John shot out of bed and came to her. "What's wrong? Talk to me?"

"They found me." She crossed her arms over her stomach and struggled to pull in a full breath. "I didn't think they'd be able to find me here, but they did."

John wrapped her in his arms.

"Why don't you read the letter before you get upset? Come on. Let's get dressed. I'll put on a pot of coffee and you can read your letter."

Without another word they donned their clothes and went into the kitchen. John grabbed his coat and pulled the letter from the inside pocket of his coat.

"Here you go." He handed her the envelope.

Lena took the letter from John with two shaky fingers. Was she afraid of what lay inside? Heck yes!

She got a knife and sliced open the top of the envelope, before pulling out several sheets of paper. The top one was a letter that she began to read silently.

April 9, 1887

Dear Miss DuBois,

My name is Jacob Goldstein and I am the attorney for Robert James Drummond, your father. Before I go any farther you should know that Mellisande DuBois and Robert Drummond were married approximately six years ago. This makes you the legitimate daughter of Mr. and Mrs. Drummond and as such you are also his heir.

She stopped reading. "It's about my father's will. I barely met the man, why would he make me his heir, daughter or not?" She shook her head and continued reading the missive.

Also, your father wanted to apologize for frightening you so and tried to make amends. He is the one who hired the Pinkerton Detective Agency to find you. I must admit you gave them a run for their money. Only a few weeks ago did they provide your father with the information as to your whereabouts. He told no one but me.

I now have the unenviable task of informing you that your father has passed away. I have followed all of his instructions for his bequests and distributed those funds and properties. I have enclosed a copy of your father's will for your perusal.

I am now arranging for the sale of the remaining business interests per his instructions. He agreed ahead of time to the sale of these assets in the event of his death. The buyers have all been notified, and the money is being transferred to an account in your name.

By the time all the transactions are complete, it is estimated that your fortune will be approximately ten million dollars. I have several financial advisors available to help you invest the money, if that is your wish.

"Oh, my God. Oh, my God. John we're rich. I mean really rich."

Lena's hands were shaking so much she dropped the letter but didn't realize it until John handed it back to her.

"Lena, honey, keep reading. Please?"

"I will finish, but you can already see our lives are about to change."

I do understand that now you are married. It is also my understanding that you chose this marriage to spite your father and his attempt to arrange a marriage for you. If you desire your marriage can be annulled or you can obtain a divorce, if you desire. You can also choose to remain Mrs. John Thorpe of Homestead Canyon.

What I'm trying to tell you is you have the world in your hands, and you may shape it any way you like.

You should come to New York City to sign various documents. If however you would prefer, I will, if necessary, send them by mail or by courier, and you may send them back the same way. I would hire a Pinkerton to do this service as they are the most trustworthy. The situation would simply be much easier if you came here. Or I can come there, if that would be more acceptable to you.

Please instruct me what you would like done. For the next year I am in your employ, per your father's wishes. My wages have already been paid for that period of time. Should you desire my services beyond April 1, 1888, we can discuss the situation at a later date.

I would also like to take this time to warn you of Mr. Rappaport. He did not take the fact of not being your father's heir very well at all. In my opinion, he is a very sly person, and he will undoubtedly find you and try something nefarious in order to get his hands on the money. BE VERY WARY OF THIS MAN. I cannot warn you strongly enough of his lack of moral fiber and his seemingly desperate nature at the reading of the will.

Please be safe. I have let no one, not even your

mother, know where you are, but if your father could hire a Pinkerton to find you then others can, too.

Yours sincerely,

Jacob Goldstein

Attorney at Law

"*L*ena? Tell me what you want to do."

"I... me... we... Oh my God." With her heart pounding so hard, there were spots before her eyes. She ran to the living room and sat in her rocker.

John followed and sat in his.

She gazed at her handsome husband. How in the world can I tell him? What will he think of me when he knows the full truth about my mother, my father and me? Regardless that they are married now, I was and will always be the bastard of a whore? Will he still want to be married to me if he knows?

Her hands shook. She could lie to him. He couldn't read the letter anyway, but that wasn't in her nature. She always tried to tell the truth and do the right thing. She hadn't lied to John; she just hadn't told him everything.

"It's a letter from my father's attorney."

"The father you met for the first time a couple of months ago?"

"Yes. He's dead. He didn't look sick, but instead quite robust. He must have had an accident, or someone killed him. He definitely didn't die from natural causes."

"Your father died?"

She nodded, glancing at the letter she still held in her hand.

John ran a hand behind his neck. "What does the letter say?"

Lena took a deep breath. "My father was, apparently, a very rich man. He left instructions that all of his business interests were to be sold and the cash be given to me."

"All right," John said slowly. "How much money are we talking here? A few thousand dollars?"

Lena shook her head.

"A few hundred thousand? You did say he was very rich."

Again Lena shook her head. She simply couldn't get herself to say the actual words.

"A million?" John's eyebrows headed for the sky.

"No. More." she said finally. "Ten million give or take a hundred thousand."

John sank back in his chair and got very quiet. "What will you do?"

"I don't know." What will we do with all that money? Should we go to New York to sign the papers? The trip would be good for John. He's never been to a large city and you can't get any bigger than New York. Oh Lord, what are we going to do?

"When you decide, let me know."

With sudden clarity, she understood John's mood. She put her hand on the arm he rested on the nearby table.

"I don't plan on divorcing you. I'm afraid you're stuck with me... for better or worse, for richer or poorer. I take my wedding vows seriously."

He let out a pent-up breath and stood pulling her up into his arms.

"Thank God."

"John, what are *we* going to do? I don't know anything about having money like that. When I started on this journey, I had just over one thousand dollars. It took me five years to save that money, and that was only because the school provided room and board."

"And you never knew your father, so you wouldn't have known he was so rich."

"That's true. My mother certainly never told me. The attorney, Mr. Goldstein, mentions my father's stepson, Eric Rappaport, and tells me to be wary of him. I went to school with him and I remember him. As a boy he tortured me, he was just mean all the time, up until we graduated. Since that time, I haven't seen him, thank God. I learned from my students that you don't grow out of that kind of personality."

"What about your mother? Can you call on her for help?"

"No," she said the single word too sharply. On a softer note she added, "I won't call on my mother for anything."

If John thought anything odd about her response to the suggestion of her mother, he didn't mention it. She laid her head on his shoulder.

He squeezed her shoulders with his arm and rested his head on top of hers

"We'll worry about Eric Rappaport later. Cross that bridge when we come to it."

She hoped they never had to cross that bridge, but she knew in her heart that Eric would come for her, or rather the money. Neither she nor John was safe.

For the first week or so, she and John talked each evening about what they wanted to do with the money.

"We could travel. Where would you like to go? We can go anywhere." Lena rested her head on John's chest.

"I don't care where we go as long as we travel together."

"Of course, we'll go together. You really think I'd let you stay behind. Some girl would snap you up."

"Flattery will get you everywhere." He turned her over and kissed her before making love to her again.

CHAPTER SIX

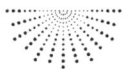

*A*lmost one month had passed since she'd received the letter from Mr. Goldstein about her father. She and John still hadn't decided what to do with all that money. More money than either of them could fathom. They had talked and talked about what to do with it but hadn't come to any conclusion. Not that it mattered; the situation was such that they could wait.

She had decided to have the papers sent to her rather than travel to New York. John wasn't ready to venture that far a field, and so Mr. Goldstein came to them.

Sam Bowmen stopped in front of their house. That in itself was unusual, but then a man in a long traveling coat and bowler hat got off the wagon and came toward her home. Lena saw this through the closet window and hurried to put her dress on.

A knock sounded on the front door.

Lena opened the door. "May I help you?"

"Helena DuBois Thorpe?"

"Yes, and you are?"

"Jacob Goldstein. May I come in?"

Lena opened the door wide.

"Of course, Mr. Goldstein, please come in."

"It is quite the journey to get to this little outpost in the wilderness that you call home."

"Obviously not far enough though, because you found me. Don't misunderstand me, I'm glad you did, but I had hoped I wouldn't be found by my father or mother. You said they married. I'm glad to hear that. I hope they had some happiness before he passed away. I'm sorry I'm being a terrible hostess. Let me have your coat and then have a seat at the table and we can go over the papers you brought with you."

Mr. Goldstein was a man of average height and weight. His hair was dark blonde with a touch of gray, parted in the middle and slicked down flat. He sat at the table and opened the case he carried.

Lena put his hat and coat on the bed and then returned to the main room.

"Would you like a cup of coffee, Mr. Goldstein? Or perhaps a cup of tea?"

"Tea would be lovely. Thank you."

She pulled two cups from the cupboard and then got down her precious china tea container that she'd bought in Denver and put a measure of leaves in each cup.

Lena had learned to keep a metal bucket of hot water on the stove at all times for washing and for occasions like this one, for tea. She dipped the steaming liquid into the cups and took them to the table.

"Before we get started can you tell me how my mother is holding up?"

"Mellisande is a very strong woman, and she's doing what must be done. She sent a letter with me for you."

He took an envelope from his stack of papers.

Lena took the envelope and set it aside.

"I'll read this later."

Mr. Goldstein nodded.

"Shall we get started? I have several documents for you to read and sign. Mr. Davis said that he will be in town for about two hours before starting back to Hanover."

"If we don't finish I'll have John take you in the morning."

"There's no reason we shouldn't finish in that amount of time. The paperwork that I have for you is very straightforward."

One and one-half hours later, Lena signed the last paper.

"Everything your father bequeathed you is now in your name. I'll file these papers when I get back to New York."

Mr. Goldstein gathered the documents together and put them back in his case.

"Thank you so much for coming out here. If you could have ten thousand dollars wired to the bank in Hanover, I'd appreciate it. You can wire it to my husband's account. John Thorpe."

The door opened and John entered.

"Did I hear my name mentioned?"

Lena stood and rushed to John. She took his heavy sheepskin coat and Stetson hat.

"John, this is Mr. Jacob Goldstein. We've just finished with all the paperwork that will transfer my father's assets to me. And I've asked him to have ten thousand dollars transferred to your account in Hanover, so we will have it to travel when we decide where to go."

John extended his hand. "Mr. Goldstein, I'm very pleased to meet you. Thank you for making this trip."

"I'd say it was my pleasure, and the trip has been interesting. The country is beautiful, but I admit the travel was uncomfortable for the most part even on the train."

"I know. Wouldn't it be nice to have our own train car? We could put in soft chairs and dining table, even a kitchen for preparing food. I've seen them. They can be quite plush." Lena put John's coat and hat on the pegs behind the door.

"It was nice to meet you, Mr. Thorpe, however I must leave now. I'm to meet Mr. Davis at the store for my ride back to Hanover. I have train tickets for two days from now."

"Thank you again Mr. Goldstein. Have a safe trip," said Lena.

"Yes, do have a safe journey," said John.

Later that night after John was asleep, Lena opened the letter from her mother.

May 1, 1887

My dearest daughter,

I'm so sorry that you felt you had to run from your father and I. The way he broke the news to you about your parentage was not well done and to top it off with the announcement that a husband had been found for you... well, I don't really blame you for your reaction. But that is all water under the bridge.

I miss my Robert every day. I still have trouble believing that he is really gone forever. I do not believe that his death was from natural causes. I believe that he was murdered by Eric Rappaport, but I can't prove it. The method I believe to be poison, what kind I don't know. I do know that I don't eat or drink anything that he has touched.

Tomorrow I'm returning to New Orleans and I hope that you will visit me there. I know how you feel about my occupation, but the house is in the Garden District far removed from my business interests. Bring your husband. I would love to meet the man that my Helena chose to marry.

I love you my dearest. You may not have believed that, growing up in the school as you did, but I do and always have had your best interests at heart. If I could have kept you with me, I would have. The hardest thing I have ever had to do was say goodbye to you at the school. I hope one day that you will forgive me.

With all my love,

Mother

Tears rolled uncheck from her eyes. Lena had always hoped but never really known if her mother loved her or not. Her love was the only thing that Lena ever desired from Mellisande. Now that she knew, she was determined to somehow see her again. That would mean telling John about her and she wasn't ready to do that. Their marriage was too new. She hoped that by now he realized that she was just the right woman for him. That she was of good moral character and worthy of his love, but she wasn't willing to test it. Not yet.

*S*ince the first letter from Mr. Goldstein had come, she'd been on pins and needles wondering when Eric would show up. She figured he would it was just a matter of time. If one Pinkerton could find her, so could a second.

Tonight, Lena sat in her rocker in the living room her mind filled with everything but her knitting. She'd already dropped several stitches and had to unravel and redo her project more than once. Cornelia Goode was teaching her how to knit and Lena wanted this, her first project to be perfect, even though she knew that was unlikely.

Not much furniture was in this room. The two rockers—sitting on a braided rug with a table holding a kerosene lamp between the chairs—faced the dining area and the fireplace. John had built bookshelves on the walls on either side. They were half full of books, all of them hers, and there was a window centered in the wall behind them. She put down her knitting and stopped rocking.

"John, I want you to teach me how to ride and how to drive the buckboard."

He raised his eyebrows. "Why?"

"Well, the buckboard, so that I can pick up supplies on my own if I need to. And how to ride, so I can go look for wild berries, or you and I could ride and have a picnic in the hills."

John laid *Moby Dick* in his lap.

They'd already read it together, so he recognized the words and understood them.

He leaned forward. "I'm not letting you go to Hanover by yourself, and I'm here to protect you so you don't have to defend yourself."

"Don't be ridiculous. I would never suggest that I go to Hanover alone. Just to the store here in Homestead Canyon. I can pick up the flour, sugar, coffee, tea and so forth without you having to come along."

He frowned. "Don't you like me to go with you?"

Then he cocked his eyebrow in that way that made her melt inside.

She stood, put her hands on her hips and blew a stray bit of hair from her eyes. "Yes, but that is not the point."

"What is the point?"

He sat back in his rocking chair, puffed on his pipe, and then blew smoke rings. After he was done, he grinned up at her.

"You want to be more independent?"

"Yes. When I need flour, I want to be able to get it now instead of waiting for you to get it on Saturday."

"You can't harness the team; you're too small and weak."

She jutted out her chin. "I'm plenty strong. Don't you have a single harness for just one horse? I could do that and…"

He crossed his arms over his chest. "How do you plan on getting the supplies into the house? You can't carry fifty pounds of flour or sugar."

"So, I'll get twenty-five pounds, which I can carry. Please John. Do this for me."

He was silent for a minute and finally said. "All right, I'll teach you."

"And to ride a horse."

He sighed. "Yes, to ride a horse."

With that sound, Lena knew she'd won.

She went to him, sat on his lap, put her arms around his neck, and kissed him.

"Now was that so difficult… saying yes to your wife?"

He slipped his arms around her waist. "If I'd known doing so would get her in my lap, I'd have said so sooner."

Lena kissed John, happier than she'd been in a long time. Her heart sang and she knew she was falling in love with her husband. *Will he still want me if he finds out about Mellisande?*

CHAPTER SEVEN

The next day, though he grumbled a bit, John harnessed his buckskin mare to the buckboard and proceeded to teach Lena to drive. He sat next to her and demonstrated as they drove back and forth on the hard-packed road in front of the cabin.

"All right. To begin with, take off the brake. You must remember to put the brake on when you stop. It won't keep the animals from moving the wagon if they really want to, but the drag will remind them they aren't supposed to."

"Right. Release the brake."

John smiled.

She supposed his expression was at her enthusiasm.

"Take the reins and slap them hard on the rear ends of the horse or horses. That will get them moving. They'll want to stop and eat but you need to keep them moving. So, if they try to stop, jerk back on the reins and then slap them on the rumps again."

He showed her how to do this and then handed her the reins.

"Let's see if you can do the things that I just told you how to."

She took the straps determined to do exactly what he'd showed her.

"First, I release the handbrake. Then I slap the reins on the horse, like this."

She raised the straps and brought them down with as much force as she could. The horse began to move. Just like John said she would, the mare tried to eat the vegetation along the roadside.

Lena jerked back on the reins, making the horse raise its head. Then she slapped the animal again to keep her moving. After practicing for about a half-hour John had her stop the buckboard by the barn.

"Now, pull back on the reins, keeping a steady pressure. If she won't stop, pull harder. Once she's stopped, set the handbrake and tie the reins loosely around the brake handle.

She did as he instructed, and the horse cooperated and stopped. After she set the brake, she turned to John and grinned.

"How did I do?"

"Great. You're a quick study."

"I do try." She tilted her head down and gave him a slow wink. "I do try."

She watched her husband blush. He didn't do it very often but sometimes when she said something a little risqué or with a double entendre, he would blush furiously.

Lena giggled. Pleased she could get that reaction from him.

*A*ugust 20, 1887

*T*hree months after he'd hired someone from the Pinkerton Agency, just like, he was sure, Jacob Goldstein had, Eric had received the information he needed—Helena's location. What Helena was doing in this little out of the way place called Homestead Canyon, he couldn't begin to fathom. The Pinkerton detective said she had gone to a marriage broker, a matchmaker person and had married, but why would she marry and come to live here? After the night he'd spent in the wayfarer cabin, nearly freezing to death, even in August, he thought the town would be better. He'd been wrong. Having lived in the city all his life, he'd never seen any place like this one.

Eric slowly rode the mare he'd rented from the stable in Hanover into town. Where the road from Hanover intersected with the road to Homestead Canyon sat a house, painted gray and white. The building was especially nice, and quite large, when compared to the cabins he saw to his right.

He turned right and headed into town, passing a boarding house then a store. Across from the store was the building he was looking for. The saloon. He'd yet to see any town, large or small, that didn't have a drinking establishment of one kind or another.

Eric pulled up in front of the building and tied off his horse. Inside he saw tables scattered across the floor with no rhyme or reason. Men, most of whom he assumed were miners, sat at the tables. Two girls wandered among the tables serving drinks, sitting on laps. One had dark hair and the other, a plump girl with dishwater blonde hair. Both looked fairly clean. He might have to try out the blonde-haired one. He did like women with a bit of flesh on them.

All the men looked ragged. Apparently, mining was hard work. Something Eric didn't intend to find out about first-hand. He wasn't made for manual labor.

He strode back to where the bartender 'cleaned' the bar with a grimy towel. The action simply spread the dirt rather than taking it off.

"Whiskey, please." He put a quarter on the bar.

"Whiskey is four bits."

Eric raised his eyebrows, surprised at the high price in such a small town. He added another quarter to the one on the counter.

The barman set a shot of brown liquid in front of Eric.

He drank the fiery brew in one swallow.

"Another and leave the bottle." Eric put a five-dollar bill on the counter.

"Yes, sir—" The bartender filled the shot glass and set the half-full bottle next to it.

Eric downed the shot before turning and leaning back, resting his elbows on the bar. He surveyed the room, looking for a likely prospect or two for carrying out his instructions. Finally, he saw who he was looking for. The man looked more ragged than the others, like he'd been at this longer without striking it rich. His coat might have been black once, but was so coated with dirt, it looked brown now. His felt hat had seen better days, the brim now floppy instead of stiff.

Picking up the bottle Eric walked over to the table.

"Mind if I sit?" He studied the chair, checking to make sure there was nothing that could stick to his pants, before he sat. Finally satisfied, he seated himself.

"Suit yourself, as long as you're sharing that bottle."

The man held up his empty shot glass.

Eric filled it.

"You have my attention. What do you want?"

"I want you to kill a man."

"That can probably be arranged. Who is it you want to kill?"

"John Thorpe."

The man started laughing.

"What's so funny?" Eric's hand tightened around the neck of the bottle.

"Have you seen John Thorpe? There's a reason they call him Big John."

"No. I haven't met the man." It doesn't matter. The

old saying is the bigger they are the harder they fall. But they do fall.

"Well, I suggest you do, and then you hire a lot more people than just me to do away with him. Shooting him is just going to make him mad."

Eric thought this was a strange thing to say, but he didn't comment.

"What about his wife, Helena? Do you know her?"

"You mean, Lena? Nicer woman you'll never find. She's the sweetest little thing, and she's got Big John wrapped around her little finger. Not that any man here wouldn't give his eye teeth to trade places with John."

Eric cocked an eyebrow. "Where do I find them?"

"Blacksmith's shop is by the mine. They have a cabin on the west end of town on the mine road. But today is Saturday. Lena will be at Mrs. Goode's for cooking lessons. Hers is the cabin next to the boarding house."

Why would Helena put up with such conditions?

"How do you know where she'll be?"

"Mister," the man cocked his head. "It's a small town. Everybody knows everybody's business."

"You've been very helpful. Let's keep this conversation between us."

"You leave that bottle and a five-dollar bill, and this conversation never happened."

Eric reached in his pocket and removed a wad of bills. The first one he peeled off was a ten-dollar bill. He started to put the bill back into the stack, but the man touched Eric's arm.

"That'll do," the man said.

Taking a deep breath, Eric nodded and put the ten on the table. Then he turned and walked out of the saloon.

$$\mathcal{L}$$ena made the short trek down to Mrs. Goode's for baking lessons every Saturday morning. She wore her favorite white dress with the flower print and lace at the hem, sleeves, and bodice, and carried two baskets. One full of the ingredients she'd need for the pies and the other to carry the baked pies home.

The weather was glorious, sunshine, warm temperatures, but not too hot, just the perfect mid-August day.

Today Mrs. Goode was teaching her to make pies. Or more specifically pie crust. Mrs. Goode's pies were so good, with a wonderful flaky crust. John loved them, and Lena wanted to make him happy.

She and John hadn't talked anymore about the money. Neither one of them knew what to do. The more Lena considered it, the more she thought they should go to New York. The trip would be good for John to see some of the country. It could be like a honeymoon.

When she arrived at Cornelia Goode's, Lena put on her apron and for the next several hours she didn't think of the money or anything but making a flaky piecrust. Finally, she pulled a cherry pie from the oven. Her second attempt. The sweet treat was golden brown and looked perfect, unlike her first try which sat on the table, dark brown on one side and appearing unbaked on the other.

"Wonderful. Perfect," praised Mrs. Goode.

Mrs. Kerr clapped her hands. "Your pie looks *delicioso*."

"Thank you. I'd best be going home. I need to cook supper to go with this pie. John will be champing at the bit to get into this if I don't have supper soon."

"It's getting dark," said Cornelia. "Let me get Tyrone to walk you home."

The big man was playing catch outside with his son, Jack, and came when his mother called out the back door.

"Tyrone would you walk Lena home, please?" asked Cornelia.

"Sure, let me carry one of your baskets, Lena."

Lena handed him the pie basket, which included the 'bad' pie. Waste not want not. She and John would eat that pie as easily as the perfect one. "Thank you for walking me home, Tyrone."

"Any time."

He looked up and down the street before they took off for John and Lena's cabin at the west end of town.

They arrived without incident, not that she expected one. She walked into her home, set the pies on the table and was greeted by her husband with a kiss on the cheek that somehow turned into something else altogether. John was holding her close to him and backing toward the bedroom.

Lena placed her hands on either side of his face. "Stop. Not now. We have to talk."

He stopped but didn't let her out of his arms. "Uh oh, I don't like the sound of that."

"What I have to tell you is important."

"So, tell me. I'll take care of it, and then I'll make love to you."

She smiled at her oh-so-amorous husband. She'd like nothing better than to make love as often as he wished. But this was important. "Remember when I read you the letter from the lawyer and Mr. Goldstein stated that my father had given his stepson the hunting lodge and the New York City apartment? Well, I know Eric, and he'll be coming here, to Homestead Canyon. He'll want all the inheritance. I'm not giving him the money. I think Mr. Goldstein thought the same. Remember he said to watch out for Eric? We have a good life, food on the table, a roof over our heads, and clothes to keep us warm. But we can use that money to do good things. We can help prostitutes get out of the life, if they want, train them for other positions. We can start schools. You get the idea. We can help so much."

John nodded. "I understand and agree. Much can be done with the money and not just for others. For us, too. Having a little fun now and then will not be bad for us. We can add on to the cabin or build a new house all together. We can live in New York, or New Orleans, or wherever you want. We don't have to stay here. There are lots of options to consider. But for now, let's have some of that pie I smell."

She pulled out the burned pie first.

His jaw dropped.

"Well, this will do." His voice was full of resignation. "I'm sure next time you make a pie it will come out beautifully."

Lena could have laughed if he hadn't been trying so hard to make her feel good about the sad looking pie.

Finally, she did laugh, she couldn't help it. Then she pulled the beautiful pie out of the basket. A wide smile grew on John's face. "Now that is more like it."

Lena cut him a large slice of the golden-brown cherry pie. The burned pie was peach, and she didn't want it to go to waste. She would take the peaches out and make turnovers with the new piecrust recipe she'd learned how to do today.

"This is wonderful. You're spoiling me."

She sat at the table next to him. "John. I want to go to New York City. I think the trip would be good for us. It could be our honeymoon."

"What about my business? I can't be gone for that long. The travel would take a week there and a week back, then if we stay there for two weeks, that's a full month. I can't leave my friends and neighbors without someone to mend their tools and shoe their horses."

Crestfallen, she sagged back against the chair. Lena had been sure he'd want to go. "I understand." She stood and turned toward the kitchen to get John a cup of coffee.

He grabbed her hand. "This trip means a lot to you doesn't it?"

"It does, and I thought you would enjoy seeing the city. But it's all right we've already taken care of the paperwork for the inheritance when Mr. Goldstein came out here, so we have no reason to go... really."

He pulled her onto his lap.

"I don't want you to be upset or sad. I'll see if the blacksmith in Hanover can come here for a day or two every other week while we're gone. Just to take care of emergencies."

She wrapped her arms around his neck. "You would do that for me?"

"Yes, I would do that for you, if going to New York City is so important to you."

"Thank you. Thank you. Thank you." She kissed him all over his face where it wasn't covered by his beard.

He chuckled. "You're very easy to please."

"I am. And there is something else I want you to do to please me."

"What is that?"

"I want you to teach me how to shoot a gun."

"Whoa." He set her away from him, stood and paced. "What do you need to know that for, I'll protect you?"

"I have no doubt you'll protect me when you're here. But you can't be with me every hour of every day. I have work to do, and so do you. Just teach me."

"This has to do with that Eric character coming here, doesn't it?"

"That's part of it. I want to know how to defend myself if I'm alone."

"All right, we'll begin tomorrow."

"Thank you." She pulled him to her and kissed him thoroughly.

After supper that night, Lena and John talked about New York.

"You make the arrangements for your business as soon as you can. I'd like to be in New York by September. The temperature won't be too hot, nor will it be cold. Mid-September would be the perfect time to visit in my opinion."

"Have you been to New York?"

"Oh yes, when I was in school." She raised her gaze toward the ceiling and remembered her trips to New York. "We would take the train into the city and spend the weekend. We'd shop, see a theater performance, and then go back to the school." *That was something nice Mother did for me. She always made sure I had plenty of spending money, so I could enjoy those trips, but John doesn't need to know that… for now.*

"I guess seeing a big city once in my life would be nice."

"The experience doesn't have to be once. John we can go as often as we like. If you wanted to, you wouldn't have to shoe horses ever again, but if you want to do that, you can. We have the whole world before us, just like Mr. Goldstein said in his letter. Don't you see, we've been given the opportunity of a lifetime?"

John narrowed his eyes, the furrows between them

becoming more pronounced. "Are you that unhappy here?"

"No." *I've disappointed him with this talk of multiple trips away from here.* "I'm very happy here, and we can continue to live just like this if you want except for one thing."

"What's that?"

"I want running water, both hot and cold. I read that something called a water heater was invented last year, and I want one."

He shook his head. "We can't. I heard about them, too. Natural gas is needed to heat the water and we don't have gas. Nor are we getting it anytime soon."

"Oh, very well, but as soon as we get gas, I want a water heater."

He grinned and hugged her closer. "Yes, ma'am, and you'll get one."

"Sure you're not just saying that to stay in my good graces? So you can hold me like this?"

"Lena, I always want to hold you, but I won't lie to you."

She cringed. Wasn't she lying by not telling him about her mother? No, it wasn't a lie. She simply hadn't said anything about her mother, and that's the way she would keep it. For the sake of their marriage, she had to. She was afraid he would end the union between them. Maybe when she was sure he loved her and would forgive her, she'd tell him, but maybe not even then.

"Let's not talk about this anymore. Why don't you

give me a kiss and let me off your lap so I can get back to work."

"*I*t's Sunday, I think you can take a bit of a break on Sunday and spend the time with your poor husband."

"Very well." She forked a piece of the pie and brought it to her mouth. Then she smiled and gave it to him.

He accepted the bite, ate it and then kissed her.

"You do like to spoil me."

Spoil maybe, make him fall in love with her, certainly. Only then would he forgive her. Wouldn't he?

True to his word, John took her out back and began her lessons on how to shoot a gun. There was nothing behind their house except scrub oak, cedar and a few pine trees. No people so no chance of hurting anyone. John had their property fenced off with split rails and he set up six bottles atop the fence.

"First, never aim the gun at anyone unless you're planning on shooting them, even in jest. You never know when the weapon might discharge by accident."

"I understand."

She stood next to him while he loaded both a rifle and his six-shooter. Just the sight of the weapons made her nervous, but she'd put up with that in order to be able to protect herself from Eric.

He gave her the pistol. The gun was much heavier

than she thought it would be and she had to use both hands to hold it, but she hit two of the six bottles he'd set up as targets.

He grinned and patted her on the shoulder. "That's wonderful for your first time. You'll do better next time. Let's see if you can get the rest of them with the rifle."

The rifle was a side-loading repeating rifle. John showed her how to hold the gun before carefully handing it to her.

"Hold the stock hard against your shoulder. There's quite a kick when it fires."

He checked to see that she held it tight and then watched her fire.

She hit three bottles.

"I like the rifle better. It's easier to handle and I just feel more comfortable with it."

"Everyone has their favorite weapon, but you should know how to use both well. You won't always have your favorite with you and need to know how to use whatever weapon you have."

"All right."

"Good. Here, try the revolver again."

She took the gun, held it with two hands, aimed and fired. Again and again she practiced until she could comfortably hit five out of six each time.

John nodded. He made her reload the gun each time, so she knew how to do it on the fly. Next, he gave her back the rifle.

They were out of bottles, so John started using cans. Each round she had six targets.

After the first round, John made her load the gun herself. Then, holding the rifle tight to her shoulder and aiming carefully down the barrel, she fired and hit another five out of six. She did that several times, fire—fire—fire, six times, load and repeat. Finally, she hit six out of six three times in a row

John let her stop.

"If you can do that well every time you have to shoot, you'll be fine. Most men can't shoot that well because they don't take their time to aim and shoot. They just point and fire. Aiming is much better if you want to actually hit what you're shooting at."

Lena hoped she never had to use a weapon against another person, but at least now she was prepared.

CHAPTER EIGHT

*A*ugust 23, 1887

*S*he carefully packed the basket with all of John's favorite foods—roast beef sandwiches, potato salad, cheese, plain bread, two apples, and his favorite cherry pie.

Lena had purchased a pair of boy's denim pants, boots and shirt at the store, for riding Star.

This was the first time she'd be riding more than just around the yard, but she knew she could handle it. She and Star made a good pair. She had to hold on to the saddle horn, jump up and put her foot in the stirrup, but she could mount by herself that way. She did however, let John help her when he was of a mind to, enjoying his hands on her waist as much as he liked putting them there.

Once the basket was packed, she put in a Mason jar of milk for good measure and shut the lid.

"John," she called. "Are you ready?"

"Yes, I'm coming." He carried a blanket.

"Oh, good. I forgot that." She pointed at the quilt in his arms.

"We'll try to keep you relatively clean."

Lena burned with curiosity. "Where are you taking me?" She scanned his expression hoping this time he'll give her a clue.

"I told you. It's a secret. But you'll like it, I promise."

Lena followed John out to the yard where the horses waited already saddled. Her Star, who was all black except for the white star on her forehead and her white socks, turned her head at Lena's arrival and softly nickered. And his mount, Jasper, a beautiful red and white appaloosa stallion that was the biggest horse she'd ever seen. A good eighteen hands at the withers, John had told her. He was a big man, so he needed a big horse.

She watched him tie the basket onto his saddle and the blanket onto hers, before making sure they both had full canteens, and rain slickers. John was taking no chances on the weather catching them unaware.

When he was done, he came back to her.

"Ready?"

"I am."

He picked her up by the waist and set her in the saddle. She bet she was the only woman in Homestead Canyon whose husband could make her fly. John made sure her feet were in the stirrups properly, before he mounted Jasper.

He smiled. "Let's go."

She nodded and grinned back. Lena was so excited to finally be going on a picnic she could barely keep from bouncing in the saddle like an eager child.

They rode through town and followed the river up toward the mountains, though they were too far away to reach them in time to have a picnic. They came over the rise of the hill and Lena looked down into a pretty green valley, which was almost completely filled with a long, skinny lake.

"Is this our destination? It's beautiful."

"Nope, too exposed."

She thought that was a little strange but kept following him. He followed the lake to where the creek that filled it went through some rocks. There was enough room for horses to get through, if they walked in the stream. The rock walls were a good forty feet above her on either side. When they came out she saw two small pools with steam rising from them.

"Hot pools?"

"Yup. Fancy a hot bath, my dear?"

"Oh John," she smiled and blew a kiss. "This is the best present."

He took them around to the farthest pool.

"This is the hottest one. Perfect for us to bathe and do some swimming, too."

Lena followed John, who rode so the horses were away from the lake. She figured he didn't want them to disturb the shore and turn it to mud. Then she jumped down and hobbled Star, just like John showed her. She reached up and untied the blanket from her saddle and walked down closer to the water. She found a flat spot covered in grass about ten feet from the shore of the pool. Shaking out the pretty green patchwork quilt, she spread it upon the ground.

John hobbled his horse next to hers and brought the basket of food.

"How do you like it?"

"I love it." She walked over to him, crooked her finger so he bent down, then she put her arms around his neck and kissed him.

He wrapped his arms around her waist and straightened, their lips never parting. She wrapped her legs around him, and he kneeled taking them both to the blanket. He was careful to brace himself on his arms, so he didn't crush her.

"You are so beautiful. I'm a lucky man."

She reached up and stroked his cheek. "I'm the lucky one. I found you. You were there when I needed someone ever so much. You've loved me when I couldn't love myself."

He stiffened.

She knew immediately what had happened. She'd said love. They'd never talked about love.

"Lena, as much as I care for you, I don't love you. I won't ever love anyone again."

Shock warred with anger at his statement. "Why

would you say something like that? Of course, you will and you do, whether you realize it or not."

"No. I don't."

"Someone hurt you badly didn't they?"

He looked away from her and nodded.

"What happened?" She looked up into his eyes. Her gaze unwavering. "I think I have a right to know."

"I was engaged to my childhood sweetheart. At least I thought she was my sweetheart. On the day of our wedding, she sent me a note rather than show up for the ceremony. Until I learned how to read, I never knew what the letter said, because I couldn't let anyone else read it and have my secret exposed."

She felt a pang of sympathy for his situation. "So, what did the letter say?"

"Here, you can read it for yourself."

"You carry that thing around with you? The one reminder of what gave you so much pain? I think that's a bit foolish. Don't you?"

"Maybe. Just read it."

Dear John,

I've decided I don't want to be married, at least, not to you. I've been in love with Jeffrey Turner my whole life and recently found out he feels the same way. We are running away to California.

I never meant to hurt you and was always certain we could make a good marriage with just friendship. But I want everything. I want love.

You should wait to marry until you find a woman who makes you burn. Makes you feel inside that she is the best part of you. When you find that woman, marry her immediately—for that is love.

I wish you the best,

Nancy

Lena put aside the letter.

"You're afraid you'll get hurt again. That's understandable, but you'll come to realize I won't hurt you. If you let me in." *And if you don't find out about Mellisande and believe the worst of me because of her.*

"We'll see. I don't believe it's possible, but we'll see."

He rolled onto his back.

She leaned up on her elbow and began unbuttoning his shirt.

"Since I met you, I believe anything is possible."

"Hmpft." He closed his eyes. "What does meeting me have to do with that?"

"I never thought to find a husband when I needed one, much less one that is so kind, gentle and handsome to boot."

He rubbed up and down her back. "I never thought to find such a good woman."

Lena cringed and worked very hard not to let it show on her face. She smiled and finally worked the last button free. Pulling open his shirt, she exposed his chest and ran her fingers through the sprinkling of soft, curly dark hair. The hair on his beard was also curly but was stiffer. The skin on her face and neck was often red and a little tender after she and John made love. His kisses were a double-edged sword, enticing and hurtful at the same time.

John reached up and pulled her head to his for a soul-searing kiss. "Let's get naked. And no, I won't close my eyes. You need to get used to getting undressed in front of me."

"Hmpft. Oh, all right. I suppose it is a little ridiculous when you've seen and probably kissed every part of me."

"Quite true. Much to my delight."

She toed off her boots and unbuttoned her blouse, letting it slide down her shoulders and to the ground. Her denims, chemise, bloomers and socks soon followed. Naked as the day she was born, Lena turned and ran for the pool, splashing in until it was waist high.

She turned and called to John. "This is wonderful." Then she stretched out and swam for the other side. When she stopped, treaded water and looked back, John was splashing his way into the pool. Lena turned and swam as fast as she could.

This may have been the largest pool, but it was only about twenty-five yards across. Not a very long way at all. She was halfway when John caught her and grabbed one of her feet stopping her progress.

He pulled her down under the water. Then he let her go.

She bobbed to the surface and sputtered the water.

"What did you do that for?" She treaded water and pushed her hair back from her forehead and out of her eyes.

"So, you would stop and play."

"I'll show you play." She quickly pushed the water at him splashing him in the face.

John grinned. "Now you've got the idea, but that calls for retaliation."

"That was retaliation."

She turned to swim away, but he caught her foot and slowly pulled her back, moving hand over hand up her leg until he held her back at his chest. Then he turned her, both treading water, and kissed her.

They sank like stones.

Sputtering Lena again pushed her hair out of her face. "I'd say it's a bit dangerous for us to kiss while in water over our heads."

"I agree. I'll let you be. Enjoy the water. I'll get your rose soap."

Lena gasped. "You brought my soap? That's so sweet."

"And towels and your comb and brush. I came prepared to pamper you."

She swam close to him.

"John, you are so good to me." *I think you must love me, even though you say you don't.*

"I try. You're my wife. You should be spoiled when possible. Just like you spoil me with my favorite pie. I bet there is even one in the picnic basket."

"How did you know?" Lena grinned. "I did put in a cherry pie.

He nodded with a satisfied smile. "I thought so."

John left to fetch her rose soap.

She'd followed him to more shallow water in which to wash. After she accepted the soap, she lathered her body and then her hair, sure to clean away every speck of dirt. Then she waded into the deeper water and dived under to rinse away all the bubbles.

When she surfaced, she shook her hair back and watched John as he soaped up his big body, then his hair and beard.

He too, walked out until the water was above his waist and then dove under, surfacing next to her.

"Feel better?"

"I feel heavenly. I don't think I've ever felt so clean. The water here seems special. Thank you, this is a wonderful place."

"It's a secret place. Not many venture through the rock canyon that hides it."

She felt special having this to share with John and no other. "I won't tell anyone. It'll be our se... secret." *I wish this was the only secret I had.*

Later when they'd both had enough swimming and dressed again, Lena set out the food. She left her hair loose so it would dry faster and it hung in a golden sheet to her waist.

John loved it when she wore her hair down. He liked to run his fingers through the pale blonde tresses

She sat on the blanket with her legs crossed and ate her lunch.

John lay across the quilt from her, propped up on his elbow.

"Have I told you how beautiful you are?"

"I think you have. Several times as a matter of fact. Usually when you want to make love to me."

"Ah, but you discovered my motive, though I do believe you are beautiful whether we make love or not. So, shall we?"

"Out here in the open? You can't be serious. What if we got caught?"

"If they didn't catch us bathing, then they won't catch us now. Come, clear away this food and make love with your husband."

Lena couldn't resist. The thrill of being caught was intoxicating.

---

*A*s the afternoon sun waned, they rode home. When they arrived, Lena helped John put away the horses, rubbing them down with handfuls of clean straw, then currying them and brushing their coats of the last vestiges of dirt. Each animal was given a flake of hay and a measure of oats.

John picked up the basket of food and Lena the quilt before they walked to the house.

Tonight, was another lesson for John, reading before they went to bed. He was getting very good.

Writing was something else. Lena purchased a slate and some chalk so he could practice without paper and pencil. Before now those had been too expensive to use for writing practice and he'd gotten used to using the slate. He was having trouble with some of his letters, but he improved with each session.

He enjoyed reading *Moby Dick*, and she liked hearing him read the words, loved hearing him getting better and better, more confident with each lesson. He was progressing rapidly, perhaps because he was so motivated to learn.

After they'd read for two hours, she'd had enough. Exhaustion was working its way through her body, inch by inch.

"Time for me to go to bed. Tomorrow is ironing, since I didn't do it today, and my regular cleaning on top of that, so I'm going to bed early. You can stay here and read to your heart's desire."

The next day was Monday, usually a light workday—just dusting, sweeping the floor and pounding the rugs. She didn't mind though. Yesterday had been wonderful, and she'd double her workload any time to have another day like that.

She'd just set up the ironing board when a knock sounded at the door. She set the iron she held on to the stove to heat.

"Coming," Lena called as she patted her hair into place.

She opened the door and nearly screamed. The man standing there was the one person she'd hoped never to set eyes on again. Before her, in his black suit and black traveling coat and with a black hat covering his brown hair, was Eric Rappaport.

"Helena. So good to see you."

Her pulse raced as she wondered how soon John would be home. "What are you doing here? How did you find me? *Why* did you find me?"

He held up three fingers. "Why, I'm here to see you." He ticked off one finger. "I hired Pinkerton detectives." He lowered his second finger. "And for the money, of course." He lowered his third finger.

Hand gripping the doorknob, Lena shook her head. "That makes no sense. The attorney, Mr. Goldstein, said you got your bequest. Quite generous, considering you were of no family to Robert." Eric laughed; the sound devoid of humor. "I want *your* money, Helena."

"Don't call me that. My name is Lena and you can't have the money. You've already gotten more than you deserve. When I saw my father, he was robust and healthy. Yet, he goes back to New York, back to living with you, and is dead within a few months. Did you kill him, Eric? Given what I knew of you, I wouldn't put it past you."

He moved closer and took her arm.

"Careful what you say, *Lena*, you might say something that will make me angry, and you don't want me angry."

Lena was surprised at the strength in his vise-like grip. Where was John? Where was anyone? "Let me go. I don't care if you're angry or sad or happy. I don't care anything about you."

"That's where you're wrong, *Lena*. You should care very much how I feel. You wouldn't want anything to happen to your husband, a Mr. John Thorpe, would you?"

"John can take care of himself." She wrenched herself free and smiled. "You haven't met my husband, have you? Why don't you go to the blacksmith shop by the mine and introduce yourself? Tell him the same thing you did me and see how he responds. If you still have your front teeth, you can ride out of town and back to New York. Be happy Robert remembered you in his will at all."

She slammed the door in his face and slid the bolt home.

Lena hurried about her chores, afraid to go outside, afraid she would find Eric waiting. But she needed to feed the chickens and gather the eggs for tomorrow's breakfast.

She grabbed her basket, opened the door and looked around, ready to slam it at the first sight of Eric. Nothing. The afternoon sun made the air warm and she enjoyed being outside. She walked out to the chicken coop and still saw no one.

The coop itself was made of natural wood and was tall enough John didn't hit his head when he went inside. The structure was surrounded on all four sides by chicken wire nailed to four-inch by four-inch by eight-foot pieces of wood. She entered through the door formed in the wire with several two by four boards. The birds flocked to her like they were starving. Lena went to the grain bin on the side of the coop and filled her apron with corn kernels. She spread the grain by hand-fuls over the ground and the chickens started pecking at the food.

"Well, I never thought I'd see the day when Helena DuBois was feeding chickens."

Lena jumped at the sound of his sneering voice but refused to look up. "I'd hoped you left. Actually, I hoped you fell down a mine shaft, but I knew that was too much to wish for."

"Not until I meet your dear husband."

He stood on the outside of the coop.

Lena was sure it was so he wouldn't get droppings on his shoes.

"Then you have a long wait. He won't be home until sundown."

"I'm glad you told me, though it wasn't a very smart thing to do. What if I wanted to kidnap you?"

Her heart hammered in her chest. "I'd make so much racket everyone in Homestead Canyon would hear me."

He stood with his hands behind him. "I bet you would. No, I'll wait to talk to your husband. He may be interested to hear what I have to say about your dear mother."

She finally looked at him, more than a little alarmed. Had he guessed that she hadn't told John about Mellisande? "My mother has nothing to do with this."

He moved forward and grabbed the chicken wire with both hands.

Lena gasped and jumped back.

"Oh, but she does. You see she got the mansion and I want that, too."

With the wire between them and him not brandishing a weapon, Lena had felt fairly safe, now she wasn't so sure. Her stomach in knots, she still had to treat him as she always had, with bravery she didn't feel at this moment. "Is there anything you don't want, Eric?"

"Well, I've decided I don't want you, but I might marry you anyway, after I've made you a widow."

Could he hurt John? What if he ambushed him? No. She couldn't believe that would happen. She had to believe in her husband. "You're insane." She realized he hadn't changed from the bully he was as a child. "I will never marry you."

"Sure, you will, if you don't want me to kill Mellisande as I do your husband."

"You won't kill John. He's twice the man you are. Literally. Go away, Eric, before John comes home and swats you like the insect you are."

"Who am I swatting like an insect?"

John rounded the corner of the coop.

"And why are you feeding the chickens at this late hour?"

Lena's stomach clenched, fear that Eric would blurt out the information about her mother gripped her.

She decided to take the high road and maybe put Eric off-kilter. "This is Eric Rappaport, my father's stepson. Eric this is my husband, John Thorpe."

John looked over the man, then wiped his hand on his pants and walked over to Eric.

Eric swallowed hard as the tall, heavily muscled man that was her husband approached.

Lena enjoyed watching him crane his neck to look up at John.

John shook Eric's hand, squeezing maybe a little too tightly if the pained look on Eric's face was anything to go by.

She looked away hiding a smile.

"What brings you from New York all the way to our little out of the way town?"

John gave Eric back his hand.

Eric brought his hand up to his chest and massaged it with the other.

"I came to see Helena... er... Lena. I wanted to make sure she is happy."

John motioned for Lena to come to him.

She dropped the rest of the corn from her apron in a pile on the ground and came out of the chicken coop to John's side where he put a protective arm around her shoulder.

"As you can see, she is fine."

"I also thought we could discuss some things, perhaps about Lena's background."

"I know all I need to know about her background. Lena has told me everything."

"I see. Well you have a more open attitude about her mother than most men would."

Eric sneered the words at John, but he didn't say

more much to Lena's relief. She felt the bile in her throat return to her stomach.

"Now Mr. Rappaport, I think we've had enough of your company."

"I'll take my leave, but I'll say this much, I doubt you got the woman you thought you did."

Eric turned, walking out of the yard and back onto the road.

Lena and John watched him as he turned toward town.

John finally removed his arm from her shoulder.

"What have you not told me?"

The words were spoken softly.

"I... uh... my... oh," Her heart beat so fast she thought it would pound out of her chest. She didn't want to tell him, but she had no choice now. She couldn't lie to him. She'd never actually lied to him and she wouldn't start now.

Lena looked down, her arms wrapped around her waist. "I should have told you before, but I have never had anything to do with my mother's business."

"And what business would that be?"

She took a deep breath and hurriedly said, "My mother is Mellisande DuBois... the most famous madam in New Orleans."

"Your mother... is a whore?"

He said the words so quietly, Lena strained to hear them.

"Was... when she started out... now she's a madam and remember she and my father married six years ago."

He jammed both hands on his hips. "You are a bastard?"

Lena stood ramrod straight. "No. I am not. I was, but now that they were married, I am legitimate."

John ran his hand through his hair. "I don't know what to think about all of this."

"You know who *I* am. I never, *never* had anything to do with her business. Mellisande sent me away when I was six and I only returned home six months before you and I were married."

"I specifically requested a woman of good moral fiber."

Lena saw the accusation in his expression and pounded her chest. "And you got one."

"I need to think about this. I'm taking a walk back to the shop to clear my head."

Lena's chest ached from deep inside. She was devastated even though she'd been trying to ready herself for this event. Nothing could prepare her for the hurt or the betrayal she felt that after all this time, he didn't accept this news as just a part of her past. He knew who she was. Who she'd become since marrying him. Why was it so difficult for him to see and accept her as she was?

When John came home that night, he didn't talk to her. He moved as if in a daze and gathered his hunting equipment. If he'd only had his gun and could have shut up Eric Rappaport before he spoke, but he hadn't and even if he'd had his gun, he wasn't a murderer. He gathered everything while at the same time ignoring Lena who sat staring into the fireplace.

"You don't have to leave, John."

He didn't answer her or even acknowledge she was in the room.

"I'll leave. I won't run you out of your home."

John glared in her direction, fury on his face. "This place has nothing but bad memories. I'd rather leave."

She turned away from the fireplace and looked at him, her hands gripping the arms of the chair. "I'm sorry you feel that way. My best memories are here... with you."

He stopped packing his gear. "They were some of my best, until today. Now they are forever tainted because I wasn't making love with the kind of woman I thought I was." *I thought you were different but you're not. You're just like my mother, a whore who abandoned me when I needed her most.*

Lena stood and braced her hands on the table in front of her. "I. Am. Not. A. Whore. Nor have I ever been one. I came to you an untried virgin, and you know that."

"You could have faked that." He knew he wasn't being rational. He was so confused he didn't know what to think.

"Faked it you say. How could I fake what you felt? How could I have faked the blood on your member or on the cloth you used afterward to soothe me?"

"I don't know but you did." *You must have or I'm making the biggest mistake of my life.* "Your mother probably taught you how."

She turned her back on him. "You're an idiot. What is it that makes you so… hateful?"

"I have my reasons."

She turned to face him again. "You have excuses."

"Believe as you wish."

"Just like you are?"

He'd had enough. Picking his pack off the floor he hefted it onto his back and then grabbed his rifle. With one last look around the cabin, his beloved home until now, he walked out the door without another word.

⸻

*H*e never looked back. She watched to see if he would. Lena closed the door, went to the bedroom, lay on the bed curled into the fetal position, and cried before falling into a fitful sleep.

When she woke in the morning, she knew she'd have to leave though she didn't want to. For the last four months, this had been her home. They'd been the best times of her life. She thought she'd finally found a place she belonged.

She wondered where John slept last night. Was he warm? Was he safe? And why should she care, but she did.

Taking a deep breath, she realized she was wrong. She would always be Helena DuBois, daughter of the most famous madam in New Orleans. Maybe it was time to stop running and go home. Her mother would care for her until she was ready to travel to New York.

She would start over. Placing her hand on her stomach, she talked to the baby that grew within.

"Don't worry little one. I'll take care of you. Your father is a fool and there is no reason he needs to know about you."

Her marriage over, Lena dragged the trunks out of the barn, packed her things and then walked down to the Goodes's and asked Dean to help her load them onto the buckboard and to harness the team, not just one horse, to the wagon.

CHAPTER NINE

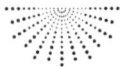

"*L*ena," said Cornelia Goode. "What do you want me to tell John when he gets back?"

"Tell him I understood and have left. I'll file for divorce when I get to New Orleans."

"Oh, no, Lena, surely things aren't that bad."

"Trust me, Cornelia, they are."

With the wagon loaded, and blankets packed for the wayfarer's cabin, water and food were the last things she got from the house.

Dean helped her up into the wagon.

She grabbed the reins, released the brake, and slapped the horses' rumps. They began to move, and she slapped them again to make them go faster. She needed to make some time if she wanted to reach the cabin before dark.

Not until Homestead Canyon was out of sight did she let the tears fall. John had totally rejected her because of what her mother did for a living. Helena had never even been to the bordello that she could remember. She must have when she was young, but even then, Mellisande was the madam, had a home away from the bordello, and only took special clients. Helena suspected, the only client she accepted was Helena's father. The two of them were very much in love, from what she knew now. Why else do you marry nearly twenty years after your child's birth?

Lena reached the cabin in plenty of time. The sun hadn't set yet, so there was light for getting water and gathering wood to replace what she was going to use.

She left the horses hitched to the wagon but watered them and fed them the hay and oats she'd brought from home. *Home.* Would she ever have somewhere she could call home again? She knew the answer. Home was where John was. She'd gone and fallen in love with her husband, more the fool, she.

She threw the bolt on the door and settled down to eat and then sleep. She hadn't gotten much rest the night before and didn't expect to get much now.

Lena lay in the bunk, looking at the underside of the bed above her, where a spider was spinning a web. She watched it for a while. The creature was making a home for her children. Lena put her hand on her stomach and felt the bump of a baby growing there. She figured that if she'd gotten pregnant when she and John made love the first time then that put her about four months along, maybe a little more. John never said anything about her thickening waistline. She was sure he thought he was being kind about her gaining weight. A child probably never occurred to him.

What would she do? She didn't want to raise her child like she'd been raised, that was for sure. No, she would keep her child with her. Teach him or her not to judge people by what others do. The child would know its mother and its grandmother, too. In these last few months, Lena realized that Mellisande had done the best she could under the circumstances. She'd provided a safe environment for Lena to grow up in, away from the stench of the bordello. Away from Mellisande as well, but that couldn't be helped. Lena knew that now.

She turned onto her side and closed her eyes. She kept seeing John's face, mottled with fury. He'd been so *angry*. She'd never seen anyone like that before. If she could, she'd take it all back. Lena touched her stomach again. No. That wasn't true. She wouldn't take any of it back. All the pain and sorrow now would soon turn to joy when her baby was here. She'd prefer that she and John raise the child together, but that wouldn't happen, and she'd better be prepared.

Lena awoke with a start, forgetting where she was. Then everything came flooding back, and she let herself grieve, crying for as long as she needed to. When she stopped, she got up and stirred the coals from the fire, poured the leftover coffee into the ashes, and stirred them again. Finally, she shoveled out the ashes into the metal bucket next to the stove that would keep any hot embers from starting a fire.

After making the cabin ready for the next person

who needed it, she went outside, climbed aboard the wagon, and slapped the reins on the horse's behinds.

"Hiya," she called to the horses. They started walking. She slapped them again, and they began to trot, once again and they galloped. She kept up that pace for about a mile then slowed to a walk for a mile or two and repeated the process all the way to Hanover. She wanted out of Wyoming and away from the memories as fast as possible.

*E*ric sat on his horse in the shadows of the falling night and watched John leave. He followed him for a while, as discreetly as he could, until John finally headed toward what appeared to be an abandoned shack far back in the forest.

John dismounted and tied his horse to the hitching rail outside the cabin, grabbed his pack, and went inside.

Eric slid from his mount and tied her to a tree. This was the opportunity he'd been waiting for. John was alone and would be back out of the cabin soon enough to take care of his horse. The only problem was the approaching darkness, which made hitting his target more difficult.

Finding a downed log about twenty-five yards from the shack, Eric set up his rifle and waited. He would kill John as soon as he emerged. An hour passed. Smoke rose from the chimney, but Thorpe didn't come outside. Another hour passed. Finally, his quarry emerged and took the reins of his horse and walked him around the side of the cabin.

If Eric wanted a clear shot, he'd have to be ready when John came back from caring for his animal. He'd kept the horse between him and Eric even though he didn't know Eric was there… waiting.

John returned, his boots crunching on the fallen branches and leaves as he rounded the side of the cabin, headed for the door.

Eric aimed as best he could and fired.

The shot missed. Dirt kicked up to the right of where John stood.

He ducked and ran for the door.

Eric fired again and missed a second time.

John ran into the cabin and the door slammed shut.

"Damn." Eric stood and walked back to his horse. He wouldn't have another opportunity now. John was forewarned and wouldn't come out until morning when he'd be able to see Eric. That wasn't good as he was sure John was a better shot. Just living out here would force John to be, if he wanted to survive.

Eric mounted and rode back to town. He wasn't going to get another chance at John, not by himself. Now though, since he knew where John was, he could send men. Three should do it.

He walked into the saloon, bought a bottle of whiskey at the bar, and then worked his way to the back-corner table. There he found Bart, the man he'd talked to when he'd first hit town. He sat at the table without being asked.

"What you want, Rappaport?"

"I want to hire you and two other men. I want to kill John Thorpe."

Bart set his glass on the table and nodded to Eric to fill it.

Eric poured the brown liquid into the glass and then put the bottle on the table next to him.

"I wondered when you might be back to see me. Me and two other guys could do it, if we could get the drop on him. He's too big to take him head on."

He moved his glass to the center of the table and raised an eyebrow. "Don't get cheap on me, Rappaport. Not if you want me to find the men you need."

Again Eric filled Bart's glass. "He's in a cabin about ten miles into the wilderness west of here, past the mine."

"I know that place. It's an abandoned miner's shack. Hunters use it now and then. From what I've heard around town, Thorpe had a big fight with his wife and walked out."

"He did, but she is no concern of yours."

"She left the day after he did. Or didn't you know that?"

"I knew, but I know where she's going. I can find her anytime I want. I need Thorpe taken care of first." *I'm happy I caused her pain. She has no right to be happy. Just as when we were children, she was a bastard. Everyone knew bastards deserved whatever grief they got.*

"It's goin' ta cost ya. Two hundred dollars. Cash. Upfront."

Eric reached into the breast pocket on his coat and pulled out his wallet. He counted out one hundred in ten-dollar bills. His money was getting low, he only had about one thousand left, but if he could get rid of Thorpe, the two hundred would be well spent.

"One hundred now and two hundred more when it's done."

Bart narrowed his eyes and huffed out a breath.

"Deal. When do you want it done?"

"As soon as possible. I want out of this town quickly. I've already been here too long."

"I know the men. For twenty dollars each they'll do just about anything."

Eric nodded and stood.

"You're a shrewd man, Bart. I expect to hear from you as soon as you're done so I can take my leave of this town."

"Understood."

Eric left the bottle with Bart and went up to the room he'd been sharing with the lovely Ruby. He'd tried first for Jolene, but she wasn't as accommodating as Ruby had been. Jolene was looking for a good man, something Eric would probably never be.

*J*ohn slammed the door shut behind him and drove the bolt home. It wouldn't prevent most people from entering but worked to keep out the animals. Now the bolt would give him time to load both weapons and prepare for the assault he was sure would happen.

Someone was trying to kill him, and he was fairly sure who. No one wanted him dead before Lena came into all that money. She'd tried to warn him about Eric Rappaport, but he'd brushed aside her concerns. Now he wished he'd paid more attention.

Once he had reloaded both the rifle and his Colt, he crawled to the back door of the cabin. Someone unfamiliar with the area, and the shack itself wouldn't know about the back door. He stepped out and peered around the side into the trees in front of the hovel.

A man in a long black traveling coat mounted a bay and rode away. Rappaport. It had to be. He wouldn't be giving up this easily if he thought he could take John on by himself. No, his only advantage had been the element of surprise, and he'd missed. Now John would be looking out for an attack.

Rappaport would not know about the other hunting site John had. He didn't really want to hunt; he just needed time away from Lena. Time to think, and hunting was as good a way to do that as any.

How could she do this to him? How could she

pretend to be the virtuous woman he believed her to be when she was just the daughter of a prostitute?

She was teaching him how to read and write. But that didn't matter. She was just like her mother, just like his mother. Oh, his mother hadn't charged for it, she simply left her ten-year-old son and his father alone and ran off with the traveling salesman. They were all the same. Women. Whores. All of them.

A small voice said, Lena wasn't like that. *She was happy with me and loved me. I should have believed her.* He ignored his small voice and went about packing his gear for another hunting place—one only he and Lena knew about. One no one would find him. The last place he should go. The last place he'd made love to his wife. The hot springs. He could stay there for months. Game was plentiful, the water helped keep the little clearing warm and he could be alone. That's what he should have remained. Alone. *But what about your friends and neighbors, the people at the mine who need your services as a blacksmith?* They didn't matter. *When Peter realizes I'm gone, and he will in a couple of days, he'll make arrangements. Right now, I think I'm going insane, otherwise how is it that I could miss her so much.*

***

*W*hen she reached the train depot, Lena paid a man to unload her trunks. Then she drove the buckboard to the livery and told the man

John would be by to pick it up, but she didn't know when. The stable owner, Amos Smith, knew John and said he'd board the horses as long as John needed to.

Lena thanked him and walked back to the train station where she bought tickets that would take her all the way to New Orleans. Back to her mother. Back to where this all started.

The train wouldn't leave until the next day, so Lena went to the Johnson's and stayed in their spare room for the night, leaving her trunks at the train station. The next day, when the train came, the stationmaster helped the conductor load the chests onto the train.

Five days and many tears later, Lena stood at her mother's home. The stately mansion did not look like the home of a bordello owner, with its four marble columns supporting a two-story portico. A swing for two was on one side of the veranda and next to it a wrought iron table and four matching chairs. A long-ago memory came flooding back of her as a little girl drinking iced tea at that table with her dolly, her nurse-maid Queenie watching from the door.

Lena brushed aside the memory, and it was replaced with the one of her father telling her he'd picked out a man for her to marry. She'd run then, too. Right into the arms of John Thorpe.

CHAPTER TEN

She mounted the stairs to the veranda, walked to the wide double doors and raised the knocker, letting it go to hear the loud 'clang' of metal on metal. The cab driver followed with one trunk, returned to the cab, and got the second trunk. She tipped him well, he dipped his head and ran back to his conveyance.

After a moment, the door opened wide and a large black man stood there. When he saw who she was, Thaddeus broke into a wide smile and welcomed her in.

"Miss Helena. We're very glad to see you. Your mama will be so happy. She's been very sad since you left." He shook an admonishing finger. "You didn't even say goodbye."

"I know, Thaddeus, and I was wrong to do that. I should have spoken to Mother before leaving. If I had…" She didn't let herself finish the thought, much less the sentence. "May I come in?"

"Of course, miss. Ah but you a missus now, ain't you? Your mama told us you got married."

The butler stepped out and picked up the valise next to Lena. "I'll send someone up with your trunks."

"Where is Mother?" She passed over the threshold into a tall, two-story foyer, with a grand marble staircase directly to her right and a hallway, thickly carpeted with oriental rugs to her left.

"She's not home from her work yet. Let me get you settled in your room, and then I'll send someone to let her know you're here."

"Thank you, I'd like that. I'm weary from more than a week of travel I've just endured."

Lena followed Thaddeus up the stairs and then down the hall to her bedroom. He was as big as John. Thaddeus was her mother's bodyguard as well as her butler.

Years ago, when her mother acquired the Negroes at the auctions, Mellisande immediately set them free, gave them the paperwork that showed them as free men and women. Then she asked them to stay with her. She paid them fairly and provided room and board as well. None of the people she acquired turned her down. Lena had always admired her mother for that attitude.

Thaddeus put the valise next to the closet.

"If you need anything you just call on old Thaddeus."

"Thank you. I will."

The butler left the room shutting the door behind him.

Lena's room hadn't changed since she'd insisted on

pink when she was a little girl. Her mother had said, "Why not?" and had the room painted and papered in various shades. The walls were a pale pink with striped wallpaper depicting dark roses on a pink background for one stripe and the solid color on the next. The curtains were brocade matching the flowers on the wallpaper, and the carpet was a deep rose color.

Her white four-poster bed with a canopy of the same material as the curtains was along one wall with matching white night stands on either side. A tallboy dresser and six-drawer bureau were on one wall, a basin and pitcher on top of the bureau.

The wall with the closet was to her right. She opened the door and walked in. All her clothes she'd left behind hung on rods inside. She wouldn't wear them right now, but they would be quite serviceable after the baby was born. Just because she now had money to buy anything and everything didn't mean she was to become a spendthrift.

She wondered what John would think of her rooms. They were as big as his entire cabin and through her closet was a bathroom including a flush toilet, and a bathtub with running water. A small stove was tucked in the corner to heat water, so the liquid was as hot as possible when the tub was filled.

That's what she wanted now, a bath, a long, leisurely bath with sweet smelling salts and lots of bubbles. Lena walked back to her bedroom and pulled the bell cord. Having someone to pour her a bath was such a luxury. After having to take a bath in a metal tub and doing everything for herself for the last four months, she didn't think she'd ever take such things for granted again.

A few minutes later, a young woman she didn't know appeared.

"Yes, ma'am, what can I do for you?"

"Hello. What's your name?"

"Leota, ma'am."

"Well, Leota, please draw me a bath, very hot with lots of rose scented bath salts."

"Yes, ma'am. Right away."

The girl, a pretty mulatto, if the golden color of her skin was any indication, nodded and hurried to do Lena's bidding.

Half an hour later, Lena reclined in the tub and let all the weariness flow out of her body. By the time she'd been in the tub for thirty minutes, the water was cold and her fingers were wrinkled.

Lena rose from the bath, feeling like she could finally sleep, put on her nightgown, and crawled between the sheets.

When she awoke, the room was dark, and she wasn't sure what time it was. She lit the lamp on her bedside table and put on her robe to venture down to the kitchen to find something to eat. She was starving, though she hadn't gone hungry on the train. For the first day she ate the bread and cheese, she'd bought at mercantile in Hanover on her way to the train station. Then she'd gotten lunch boxes at several of the train stops along the way.

She walked through the door and saw her mother sitting at the kitchen table with Thaddeus, both with a cup of coffee and a plate of macaroons in front of them. *My favorite cookie.* Crunchy on the outside, soft and chewy on the inside, with chocolate ganache sandwiched in the middle of two cookies.

"I thought you would come here first when you awoke. Hello, *ma petite cherie.*"

Mellisande DuBois was a beautiful woman of about forty-five. She had the same pale hair color as Lena, almost white blonde.

Mellisande upgraded the brothel's women. Accepting only the most beautiful and accomplished courtesans. She also rigorously screened the clientele she accepted. The men must be rich, generous, and well-mannered. The changes made her brothel the most exclusive in New Orleans, and Mellisande a very rich woman.

"Mother, I hadn't expected to see you. Is it that late? Or that early? I didn't bother checking the clock, I was too hungry."

Mellisande laughed softly. The sound was throaty, not the tinkle you would have expected from a woman who looked so ethereal.

"Oh, my *cherie.* It is that late." Mellisande stood and opened her arms. "I am so glad you are home, but I have to ask why, when you will so obviously make me a *grandmere.*"

Lena lost all her animosity toward her mother and

only wanted to feel Mellisande's arms around her. She ran across the floor.

"Oh, Maman. I've been such a fool. He found out about you, called me a whore and left."

Her mother wrapped her in the comfort of her arms and cooed to her.

"Hush, now, *cherie*. All will be well. Hush, *ma petite enfant*."

Thaddeus quietly got up from the table, poured Lena a glass of milk and then left the two women alone.

"I have missed you so, Maman All these years, and all I wanted was to be loved by you."

Mellisande put Lena at arm's length. "Oh, but you have been. I could not raise you here in this atmosphere, or your husband would more than likely have been correct. You would have gone into the family business and been quite a success. I have no doubt. But I did not want this life for you. I wanted you to be more than I have been. To have love, real love, like I had with your father. To have that and to shout it to the world is what I wanted for you. It appears that you had found such love."

Mellisande opened her arms again and wrapped them about Lena.

Eyes brimming with tears, she rested her head against her mother's shoulder.

"Helena, how did your husband find out about me, and what I do?"

"Eric. Eric Rappaport came and threatened to tell John, so I told him myself. I'd hoped he'd fallen in love with me, too, and that it wouldn't matter, but I was mistaken."

"What do you wish to do?" Mellisande released her.

Lena sat at the table next to her mother.

"Do you want to stay here? Stay married? Divorce him? Actually, I should ask if you want to marry him in the first place. Your legal name is Helena Drummond and has been for the last six years. Your marriage *may* not be legal if you married him as Helena DuBois, which I'm sure you did, since you didn't know your father and I had married. That is something that Jacob would have to find out for you—"

"*What do you mean not be married?* Do you understand the repercussions not just with my marriage but with my work? I accepted money under a false name. I could go to jail for that. I hope that Jacob finds that my marriage is legal."

"We'll just have to wait and discover what Jacob says, but the thing you must decide regardless of the validity of your marriage is whether you want to remain married to him, legal or not. Just let me know what you would like to do and I will see it done. You can stay here as long as you like. Your father left me his mansion in New York. That might be the best place to go and wait for the baby. We will go out together and I'll see you settled before I return. While we travel, in your father's private railroad car so you will be comfortable, you can decide if you want Jacob to draw up divorce papers, assuming he says that your marriage was legal and then have them served on your husband, although I don't believe you'll have to go through all of that."

"I don't know. Can Jacob really do that? I would not have to see John then."

Mellisande smiled. "Jacob is a man of many talents and infinite discretion."

"He kept your affair and marriage to my father a secret, didn't he?"

"Yes. He did. Your papa and I have loved each other for many more than the twenty-three years you have been alive. He was my first, my very first benefactor. I fell in love with him that first day, I was fifteen. My father sold me to the old madam, and she saw in me great opportunity." Mellisande tilted her head. "For you see, like you are now, I was very beautiful."

"You are still beautiful,Maman. Stop fishing for compliments."

Mellisande chuckled. "Ah, you found me out. Yes, I miss getting compliments. I miss your father. He was my only lover after I became the madam and had total control of my clients. I chose to be with only your father and he also made that choice. Your birth was a great joy for us both.

"I kept you with me as long as I dared. But even at age six, your beauty was evident, and I knew only a few years remained before some of my shadier clientele would want me to put up your virginity for auction. I could never do that, but I thought it best to get you out of harm's way. Your father agreed to pay for your boarding school and all your expenses there. I sent you spending money, but he was responsible for seeing you through those years."

"I always thought you did that for me. I never knew him." Lena's heart was in her throat with the knowledge that she was born out of love. That her mother really did love her. *I was born of love. I never wished for more than that. My mother loves me.*

"That is what he wished. The situation with you would have been too difficult to explain to his wife because she had not been able to provide him with a child. In fact, she died in childbirth. The child as well.

"When Robert married the second time, he promised to care for his wife's son for the rest of his life. That is why Eric was even mentioned in Robert's will. He was keeping his promise."

Lena laid her hand on her mother's arm. "Maman, I believe that Eric murdered Robert, but I don't know how. When I accused him of the deed, he did not deny it, only threatened to do the same to you if I didn't give him the money."

Mellisande closed her eyes and pounded the table. "I, too, believe Eric killed Robert. Stay away from Eric. He was an evil little boy and always will be. He will never be a man no matter his age. He believed that he would be Robert's heir and would inherit everything, because you were a bastard—"

Lena nodded. "He said those very words to me."

"Yes, those are his words, my darling, not mine." Mellisande leaned forward and placed her hand on Lena's. "I wanted you from the first day I knew I was expecting you, as did your father. A child was never more wanted than you."

"I feel that way about this one," Lena touched her belly understanding at once the love her mother must have for her because she loved this baby she carried more than anything and would protect it at all costs.

"And your husband? How does he feel about *le bebe*?"

Lena sighed, put her elbow on the table and leaned her chin on her hand. "He doesn't know."

Mellisande's eyebrows shot up. "How could he not know that you are increasing? Is he blind?"

Suddenly Lena's eyes filled with tears. *Yes, John was blind. Blind to everything but his hatred.* "Of course, he's not blind. He's a blacksmith. He couldn't be blind to do that."

"But he seems to be blind in every other way. He does not recognize the love you have for him nor the wonderful woman you are nor, unless I'm greatly mistaken about your character, the fact you came to him a virgin—"

She stared with her jaw dropped. "Maman!"

"Well, you were, were you not?"

"Yes, of course I was. Even though I knew the specifics of what would happen when we became lovers, John waited until I was ready. He is a very considerate lover."

"If he didn't know the difference, then he is a stupid man and a terrible lover."

Lena sighed. "I thought he was a wonderful lover, but he said that virginity can be faked."

"*Mais non*." Mellisande waved her hand in the air. "He is a stupid man. Only an idiot would think that real virginity can be faked."

"I'm a terrible wife. I should be disagreeing with you, but I do believe he's being stupid about this."

"How could he not know you are *avec un enfant*? I could see that immediately. You have put on some weight and it looks wonderful on you. You practically glow and would do so if you were happier."

"I believe he thought he was being kind by not mentioning my weight gain. I don't think having a baby ever occurred to him."

Mellisande rolled her eyes and shook her head. "I cannot believe the stupidity of some men. Oh well. We will stay here long enough for you to get your strength back, and then we will travel to New York and stay in the mansion until the baby comes. Don't worry the time will pass quickly, and you and I will get to know each other."

Lena reached over, put her hand on her mother's and squeezed. "Thank you, Maman."

"Always, *ma bebe*. Always."

CHAPTER ELEVEN

*B*art had to wait several weeks before the men he wanted to help him carry out the contract on John Thorpe, arrived at the mine. He'd known they were coming he just didn't know when. He could almost taste the money… well the whiskey the money would buy.

Earl Spenser and Henry Otterman were tall men and anxious for the promised payday.

"When do we do this? I want my money now." Otterman slammed his fist on the table.

They sat at Bart's regular table in the back corner of the Homestead Canyon Saloon.

"Calm down, Henry," said Bart, his voice low. He poured the man a drink. "And stop making so much noise. I don't want every man in here to know our business."

"Sorry, Bart," whispered Henry. He greedily took the shot glass and downed the drink in one gulp.

Henry Otterman was totally bald, about six-and-a-half feet tall, and heavy. The man had never missed a meal.

Earl Spenser, younger than Henry by a decade, had dirty blond hair, was almost as tall as Henry, but slender, wiry.

Bart poured the men a drink from his bottle. He wanted both men sober, so he dared not put the bottle on the table and let the men pour it themselves.

"I'll give you each ten dollars now and ten more when the job is done."

Bart put a ten-dollar bill on the table in front of each man.

Earl and Henry both snatched up the ten and put them in their pockets.

"Where do we find him? He ain't been at his blacksmith shop for a couple of weeks."

"He's hunting. You know the old Orndorr place?"

Both men nodded.

"That's where he's holed up."

Earl laughed. "Heard he's hiding from his old lady."

"He's not hiding," said Henry. "He said he went hunting. I don't guess she believed him. Packed up and left the day after he did. Only, she went to Hanover."

"It makes no...never mind about his wife. I'm only interested in him. I want him dead. Can you do that?" Bart asked.

"Sure, Bart." Earl downed the whiskey in his glass. "Give us a couple of days to get our stuff together, and then we'll all three go. To kill John Thorpe will take all of us. None of us is a good enough shot to take him out that way."

Bart took a deep breath, leaned forward and glared at each man. "You don't need a couple of days unless you think to run, but ten dollars isn't enough money to run on. You've got until tomorrow morning, then you'd better be here. Or there'll be hell to pay. You understand?"

"Sure, Bart, sure." Henry reached for the bottle. "First, gimme a drink. I need to get my courage up. John Thorpe is a mountain of a man, even for me, and I ain't no shrinking violet."

"There'll be three of us," said Earl. "We can take him. He's not invincible."

Early the next morning, before the sun had risen, the three men set out for the Orndorr place. Just a rundown shack on a few acres. The Orndorrs came out looking for gold in the sixties, but never found any. Now their place was used by hunters or others just traveling by and needing a place to sleep or to stay dry in a storm.

Bart, Earl and Henry arrived at the cabin about eight o'clock. As they expected, John was gone.

"Set up. Go hide those horses, Earl. Henry, you get in place on the back side of that door. You'll have the drop on him when he comes in. When Earl gets back he'll be on this side of the door and I'll be over by the fireplace."

Finally, they were all ready and waiting for John to return. There was no guarantee he would. He could be out tracking a deer and not be back for days or he could come back in a few minutes.

As it turned out, they only had to wait a few hours.

John entered the clearing in front of the cabin, leading his horse, with a deer tied over the saddle. When he got to the house, he wound the reins to his horse around the hitching rail and slung the doe over his shoulders. Then he walked to a ponderosa pine tree about thirty feet from the cabin and strung up the deer to a sturdy branch to cure.

"Shh, now. He's a comin'," said Bart.

*J*ohn opened the door and immediately saw Bart. He moved to pull his pistol.

"Don't do it. You don't want to die just yet. Put your hands up."

John sighed and raised his hands. He knew he shouldn't have come back to the cabin but staying by the hot pools had been too painful. Too many memories of his last day with Lena. "You're right. Bart, isn't it?"

"Yup. Bart Newton. I got me some money to kill you, but bein' a businessman, I figure I'll see if you can pay me more not to kill you."

John stood stock still with his hands raised. He didn't want one of these yahoos to shoot him by accident because he now had something worth fighting for. Lena. He loved her more than he could fathom and didn't want to die because someone had a twitchy trigger finger. "Smart man. I've got money saved up. You and your boys here can split it any way you want. How much are you getting paid, and by who?"

"One hundred now and another two hundred after the deed is done," said Bart.

"Hey, wait a minute," said Earl. "How come you're only giving Henry and me ten dollars? It should be thirty-three. That would be equal."

"I'm the one who found the job, so I get more."

"I don't think so." Earl shifted his rifle to aim at Bart. "I think you'll share everything right now or you won't see the next light of day."

"Now Earl, let's not discuss this now. Let's just take care of him." He jutted his chin toward John.

"No. I want the money you owe us now."

"I ain't got it on me."

John cleared his throat. He didn't really need this. Maybe he'd just let them kill each other. No, he couldn't do that. "I'll give each of you one hundred dollars to let me go and tell me who paid you to kill me. Then you can get out of town without the law chasing you."

Henry spat on the floor. "He's got a point. We don't need to be on no wanted poster. Not when we can make money without it."

Bart lowered his rifle, and so did Henry and Earl.

"You got a deal. John Thorpe," said Bart.

"Who hired you?"

"Some dandy been hanging around the Saloon and keeping time with Ruby, name of Rappaport. Eric Rappaport."

He knew it. Eric Rappaport. He might have to kill that man. "Come with me boys and I'll get your money."

"You're not gonna try and cheat us out of it?"

John squared his shoulders. "I'm an honorable man. I pay my debts."

He walked outside to his horse, followed by his three would-be murderers. These weren't bad men, just desperate. He was a good judge of character, at least he thought he was... until Lena. How could he have been so wrong about her?

You weren't wrong, said a small voice. Lena is a good woman. You were wrong to blame her for your mother's failings. Lena is not your mother, and she is not her mother. She is Lena.

John didn't want to think about it anymore. He couldn't have been wrong twice... could he?

John rode toward Homestead Canyon and then turned off toward the mine. Peter Van Dyke had a safe there and let the town's businesspeople use it.

Peter was outside the office building when John and company pulled to a halt.

"Well, what are you doing here? Last I heard you were hunting."

"I need to get my money, Peter. I owe these men."

"Sure. Sure."

The safe was in Peter's office.

"You all wait here, and I'll get your pouch, John."

Peter walked into his office and closed the door

behind him. A few minutes later he came out with a long leather pouch.

John reached in and took out three hundred dollars in twenty-dollar gold pieces. He gave each man five of the shiny coins.

"Now, if you boys are smart, you'll take that money and leave town."

He narrowed his eyes and lowered his head.

"I don't want to see any of your faces around here. Ever. Consider yourselves lucky, I didn't break your necks for what you tried to pull."

"Yes, sir, Mr. Thorpe. John. We're leaving town now," said Bart as he pocketed the coins.

The three men ran to their horses and took off down the road toward Homestead Canyon.

Peter Van Dyke leaned against the doorframe to his office.

"What's going on, John? You've been gone for almost two months and I get the feeling that if those yahoos hadn't tried to kill you that you'd still be gone."

"How'd you know they tried to kill me?"

"What else would you be paying them one hundred dollars each for?"

John reached up and ran a hand along the back of his neck.

"You're right, I said I'd pay them more. Lucky for me, they thought that was a good idea."

"Only smart thing any one of them has probably ever done."

More than anything, John wanted to go home to his wife. He knew he'd been wrong to judge her. His time alone had taught him he shouldn't rush to judgment, and maybe he should trust his wife. "Have you talked to Lena?"

"You haven't been home, I take it."

"No. I came straight here so I could pay those clod hoppers."

"Lena's gone. She left the day after you did."

John raised his eyebrows. "What? Where?" Then he remembered she'd said she should be the one to leave.

"I don't know. You might get more information out of Cornelia Goode. I think she was the last to see Lena."

John rode home slumping in his saddle, after his sojourn in the mountains, knowing Lena was gone.

He walked in and, if he hadn't already known, he would have then. The house was neat as a pin, but there was a visible layer of dust on everything.

He walked into the bedroom, opened the closet, and saw that all her clothes were missing. He sat on the bed and hung his head. There hadn't been enough money in the cookie jar for her to have survived for long. He'd gone off and left her, abandoned her, how could he expect her to still be there after all this time?

When he left he'd been so angry. Never had he felt so betrayed, but the longer he was away and the rage subsided, he realized Lena had never actually lied to him. She had never told him a story about her mother.

And she had been a virgin when she came to him. Now he couldn't believe the words he'd shouted in anger, that her virginity could be faked. If she hadn't before, she would have known he was an idiot with that assertion.

"Finally decided to come home, did you? Finally decided to see what your anger had wrought?"

John looked up to see Cornelia Goode standing in the doorway, arms folded across her chest.

"Where is she?"

"Went back home. Said to tell you she understood. Left the day after you did. When I came up here to find you and tell you to go after her, I saw that man who came to town looking for Lena. Name of Fric Rappaport. He took great joy out of telling me what happened. Seemed to be hoping you'd get yourself killed hunting."

John took his old carpetbag from the closet and quickly packed some clothes in it.

"He did his best to make sure I did just that, but he missed. I've got to find her. I've got to get her back. Oh, Cornelia, I've been such a fool."

"I could have told you that."

"Excuse me, but I've got to go."

She stepped aside, let him pass and then followed him out the door, shutting it behind her.

"I wish you luck, John. I think you'll need it."

He hurried out and re-saddled Jasper, his big red appaloosa and lit out toward Hanover. He had his moneybag with him and would get on the first train out of Hanover. He had months to make up for. If only Lena would forgive him.

CHAPTER TWELVE

*E*ric waited in Homestead Canyon for John's return. The three men he thought he'd hired were unreliable. Bart had instead absconded with the one hundred dollars never to be seen again.

Eric knew he didn't have any chance of getting the inheritance if the big man was alive. He'd watched their cabin for signs of occupancy but hadn't seen any comings or goings since Lena left. So, he was surprised to see Mrs. Goode walking inside when he arrived for his daily check.

He was even more surprised to see John Thorpe, beard long and shaggy, hair wild, run out to the barn for his horse. When he spotted John riding out leaving Mrs. Goode standing beside the cabin watching him, Eric knew he'd found out about Lena.

Eric ran back to the saloon where he'd been keeping Ruby, busy for the last two months, packed his clothes and followed John as fast as the horse he'd rented in Hanover would go. The mare wasn't anything like the magnificent stallion John rode, but Eric knew he'd be able to catch Thorpe at the wayfarer's cabin.

When he finally got the cabin in sight, he was surprised no horse stood out in front. He rode in and discovered the place was empty. Apparently, Thorpe had gone on riding through the night. In no way Eric, who didn't know the country, could continue. He pulled his horse to a stop outside the cabin and went inside until the morning's light.

ⅉ ohn rode like the devil was after him. He knew the way to Hanover, and so did Jasper. He rode through the night, with help from a moon bright enough to show him the way.

He arrived in Hanover early the morning after he left Homestead Canyon. Fifty miles had never seemed so long, and yet he covered the distance faster than he ever had before, in only ten hours. He'd pushed Jasper as hard as he could without injuring the stallion.

Upon arriving, he went directly to the stables and talked to Amos Smith.

"I need you to keep Jasper until you hear from me."

"I can do that, but I still got your buckboard and team from the missus. You want me to keep them too or sell them? I've had a couple of offers."

"Keep them, please, Amos. I'll pay you for them. I got seventy-five dollars here that should take care of them for a while." John pulled out his money pouch and paid Amos.

"Sure thing. You going after the missus?"

"Yeah—" John ran his hand behind his neck, but it did nothing to stop the burning in his gut. "I've done some stupid things in my life, but none were as bad as what I did with Lena. I hope she'll take me back."

Amos slapped the big man on the back. "You're a good man, John. Just make sure you remind her of that fact. And tell her you love her."

"I wasn't sure before, but I do love her." The tightness in his throat at that revelation made it difficult to speak. "That's what makes what I did that much worse."

"You'll work it out."

"See ya, Amos."

John went to the bank and got the rest of his money. He didn't know how long he'd need to be anywhere while he convinced Lena to forgive him, but he would be prepared. With what was left of the cash he'd had in Van Dyke's safe and the money at the bank, he had more than seven hundred dollars saved. That should last him a little while, anyway.

At the train station, he bought tickets for New Orleans. He didn't know where to go after he got there but figured he could find the place. Lena said her mother was the most famous madam in New Orleans. A few questions would set him on the right track.

His luck was holding. The train he needed would be leaving that afternoon. He had time to get a bath and a haircut. He'd also decided to shave off his beard. He didn't want to give Lena whisker burn.

John thought of how delicate her skin was and how she never complained when he left her face tender from kissing her with his full beard. He'd had the beard for so long his face would be white where it had been, but that didn't matter.

First, he went to the bathhouse. The place was a small four-room building; the front held two bathing rooms—one for men and one for women and a third room was for shaves and haircuts. The fourth room in the back was where the owner lived.

The trip to the bathhouse revived him and his spirits. He was surer than ever that if he apologized and asked for a second chance, Lena might give it to him. If she'd only listen to him. He'd grovel if she wanted him to. He'd finally come to realize, while he was alone with his thoughts in the wilderness, she was the most important person in the world to him. Now to figure out how to prove it to her.

The train ride to New Orleans was torture for John. He was too big for the padded wooden seats in the train cars. The best fit he had was the front seat which had a little more legroom. He took up two regular spaces. On routes that were full, he got a lot of angry looks. If he saw a woman was left standing, he rose and allowed her to have a seat. He would stand or lean against the wall until finally, on the last leg of the trip, the conductor let him ride in the baggage car where he could sit on a trunk and stretch his legs at the same time.

When he got off the train, he asked the stationmaster for the location of Mellisande DuBois.

The man smiled wide. "You *are* here for a good time. Her establishment is at the corner of Rampart and Music Streets."

John hailed a cab to the address the depot master provided. The bordello was two stories tall with a balcony around the upper level. He assumed it was used by the girls, if they wished, to put their wares on display in relative safety. The pale green building had white trim and was quite attractive. From the outside John would never have known it was a bordello. That, he assumed, was the point.

He knocked and was greeted by a large black man who crossed his arms in front of him.

"What can I do for you, mister?"

"I need to see Mellisande DuBois."

"Miz DuBois does not take clients any longer."

"No, I'm not here as a client, I'm her son-in-law."

The man put down his arms and extended a hand.

"I'm Leon, sir. I'm the, uh, butler for Miz DuBois while Thaddeus is in New York City. Miz DuBois is in her office in the back. If you'll follow me."

John trailed the man down a lushly carpeted hallway to a dark wooden door. He wondered if this was mahogany. He'd heard of the wood before but never seen it. John wanted to touch the carpet and see if it felt as soft as it looked. He'd never seen anything like this place. If where Lena lived now was anything as luxurious as this bordello was, how could he ask her to return to him? But he had to at least try.

The man knocked on the door and John heard a woman's voice say, "Enter."

This room was richly furnished. Deep blue hues dominated both the carpet and the drapes. Paint and wallpaper in light blue covered the walls where no bookshelves stood. John had never seen so many books in his life. He wondered if she had read them all. Had she been Lena, he knew the answer would be yes. His Lena loved to read. His Lena. He couldn't fathom the thought that she would be other than his Lena. The pain would be too great to bear.

John would have known Lena's mother anywhere. She looked just like Lena, from the slight stature to the white blonde hair.

"This man says he's your son-in-law. Do you want me to throw him out?"

"No, but thank you, Leon. I've been expecting him."

She narrowed her eyes and lifted an eyebrow, then came around to the front of the great oak desk.

"I was just expecting him much sooner."

"Yes, ma'am." Leon bowed and left the room closing the door behind him.

John was put off that she sounded accusatory, but then realized she had a right. "I'm sorry Miss DuBois or should I say Mrs.—"

"Mellisande, will do just fine, *monsieur.*"

"I'm John Thorpe."

The woman looked him up and down.

"My Helena said you were a big man. She did not exaggerate."

John worried the hat he held in his hand. The felt hat had seen better days, but it was the only one he had. Just like the ill-fitting black suit he wore.

"Can I see her? I have a lot to apologize for."

"Yes, you do, but Helena is not here. I've only returned last week from taking her to my home in New York City."

John slumped. He wasn't ready for another trip, but he had to get to Lena. "Then I'll have to go there. Thank you for your time."

John turned to go.

"Mr. Thorpe. Are you sure you want to woo her to continue the marriage? I'll still be a madam, this," —she gestured to the surrounding room— "is my business and how I make my living. That won't change. Can you accept that situation? I intend to be a much bigger part of Helena's life, and if you cannot adjust to me being with my daughter, then perhaps you had better stay away. Hmm?" She arched her eyebrow.

"I was wrong to judge you, ma'am." John was surprised by Mellisande. This polite, calm, attractive woman was not who he thought of when he labeled her a whore. "Lena is exactly who I want, and I don't much care what you do. That doesn't affect who we are or how we live. I will admit, I don't cotton to your line of work, but there will always be soiled doves. That is a fact of life, and one I had better accept."

"That is true, and if not for my line of work, you would never have met my Helena, for that is how I met her father. I loved him all my life. Even now, when he is gone, I love him." She swallowed hard, and he saw the moisture in her eyes. "And I miss him greatly. Are you surprised that I, *a whore*, could love so fiercely and still do what I did?"

John looked down at his hands, his hat wrung between them. He released his hat into his right hand and put it down to his side.

"I admit, I never thought it possible. I didn't think of those in your business as having feelings like the rest of us. I was seeing Lena as though she was my mother, who left me and my father for another man. My father never got over it." He looked up. "I guess I never did either."

She rolled her eyes and shook her head.

"I'm human, Mr. Thorpe. Just like you. I'm sorry for the loss of your mother, but my Helena is not her."

"Please call me John, Mrs. Drummond... I mean, Mellisande. And yes, I know that... now."

"Unfortunately for my daughter, she has fallen in love with you. If she had not, then you would not be sitting here now. I would have thrown you out. However, I know men, and I like that you have come after her, John. Even though you've hurt *ma cherie* deeply, I believe that you truly do want to make amends."

John nodded, relieved that Mellisande was at least listening to him. "I do, ma'am."

"I will help you. I was going to New York to be with Helena, anyway. I only came home to transact some business that could not be put off. You may accompany me in my private rail car. You'll be much more comfortable, and we can get to know each other a little. Helena and I found it very beneficial to be alone together for a week."

"Thank you, Mrs. Drummond. I won't let you down."

"As much as I like to hear myself called Mrs. Drummond, call me Mellisande, for we are to be family."

"I forgot. Yes, Mellisande, we are family now, and I won't take no for an answer."

Mellisande sat on one end of the settee and John on the other. Her chef, Bertrand, was traveling with them and also serving as butler for the trip.

John had never seen anything as luxurious as this rail car. It was like the living room of the finest hotel he could imagine. Carpeted in beautiful maroon, the walls were papered in a floral pattern with the small flowers echoing the color of the carpet. Halfway up the wall was a chair rail in dark wood he now knew was mahogany. The windows all had curtains that matched the deep burgundy red of the carpet.

The settee and two chairs were on one side of the car, a dining table and four padded chairs on the other. A liquor cabinet folded down from the back wall.

"Would you prefer to sleep on the settee, or would you be more comfortable with a pallet on the floor? Bertrand will prepare whichever you prefer."

Relief flooded him that she made the suggestion because he didn't know how to ask. "The sofa, while soft, is much too short for me."

Looking out the window of Mellisande's train car, John saw a very different country go by than he was used to seeing in Wyoming. He'd learned about the large cypress trees with their hanging foliage and magnolia trees with the lovely lemony smelling blossoms. As the train moved, the countryside changed, and he saw all varieties of landscapes from lush to barren.

Mellisande sat in one of the chairs with her ankles crossed. She relaxed with one arm resting on the armrest. "I will see it done. Now tell me about yourself, John. I want to know what made my Helena fall in love with you."

"I don't know. I know now that I fell in love with her the moment I saw her, though I wouldn't admit it. She was... is... bright, funny, and loving. She only tried to make me a better man. Did I tell you she would read to me like she did her students? She used different voices for each character, and the experience was like being in a theater."

"I did not know that Helena had such a talent. Please go on." She took a sip of her tea.

He sat with his legs crossed and clasped his hand in his lap hesitant and embarrassed to admit his weakness. "That was before she learned that I couldn't read and write. When she found out, instead of looking down on me, she began to teach me. And she was ever so patient about it, never once losing her temper or mocking me."

He smiled at the memory.

"I heard the same from her teachers as she grew up. She would help the younger students when they were having problems." She sat forward and waved her hand between them. "Tell me about you. You said your mother left you. What was your life like that she could ever leave her son?"

"We were poor, there is no denying that. And my father was not an easy man to get along with. I saw him hit her a couple of times."

"*Mais non.*" She shook her head and frowned. "That is never acceptable. I would have left too, but I would have taken you with me."

"I think she left when she had the chance. Father and I were out in the field, when we came back for supper, she was gone."

"Did she leave a note?"

"She couldn't read or write. My father said there was no need for learnin' except for numbers to make sure you weren't being cheated." *Why am I willing to share this with Mellisande when I never did with Lena? Lena and I never talked about our families. I guess we both had something to hide.*

"Forgive me, but your father sounds like a hard man to love, for a wife or a son."

"He was. I'm not sure I loved him. I feared him until I got big enough that he stopped even trying to use the strap on me."

She gasped, her eyebrows rising. "He beat you?"

"Yes, whenever he thought I did something wrong or when he was drunk."

Mellisande set her teacup and saucer on the short table in front of the settee. "Did you ever hurt my Helena?"

"No, I never touched her in anger. Even when the rage hit me when I found out about you, I left. I would never hurt Lena."

John picked one of the little sandwiches off the tray on the coffee table and popped it into his mouth. The cucumber crunched and was refreshing, but even the whole plate wouldn't make him feel full.

"You would never physically hurt her. That is good. Given your size, you could kill her if you struck her. But you did hurt her terribly in here." She tapped her chest.

"I know, I'm so sorry. I've never had such anger hit me before. When I thought she was..." He looked away from Mellisande, uncomfortable with the direction of the conversation.

"A whore. You can say the word." Mellisande waved her arm in front of her.

"I'm not offended. I am what I am, no more and no less. I do not apologize for what I've done, for I have my Helena, and I had great love in my life with Robert.

I cannot be sorry for anything in my life, for those paths all led me here."

"You have an odd way of looking at things. Most women would hate to be... a prostitute."

"Do not be so sure. The women in my employ have chosen this way of life. Very few of my ladies were forced into the profession, and none of the current ones. They have great beauty, but they were poor and knew that if they simply married and carried on, nothing would ever change. So, they came to me. I have trained them and each of them can leave whenever they wish. There is nothing to stop them, except the money, and most have fallen in love with their benefactors, despite my telling them to refrain from such emotions." She laughed. "I suppose I should have practiced what I preached, you're thinking."

"I admit the thought occurred to me." John picked up his cup and then reached for the coffee pot.

"Let me."

The train car swayed, and she had to pause before she poured him a fresh cup of coffee and returned the pot to the table.

"Do you regret your choices, John?"

"Some very much. I regret the way I treated Lena. I should have believed her and trusted her, but I didn't. But my greatest regret is that I told her I would never love her. I hope she will believe me now."

"You must write her a letter. You must put into it all your feelings for Lena. It must be in your own words, but I will help you with your spelling, if you need it."

"Do you have paper and pencil?"

"I have paper, pen and ink. No pencils. You will write it until you get it the way you want it and then copy the final words onto a fresh sheet of paper."

John nodded, though he didn't like being dictated to, he also realized that Mellisande was trying to help him.

"Wait here a moment." Mellisande stood, and went back to her bedroom, returning with the items needed for writing the note.

"You have four days now to determine what you want to say. Think of it like she is in the room. What would you say to her if she was here?"

She sat at the table and wrote while John spoke.

"I'd tell her I'm sorry for all the pain I caused her. That I was wrong, and that I was putting her in the same shoes as my mother. That it was my mistake. She is not my mother or her mother." He shot a glance at Mellisande, but she looked at the paper. "She is just Lena. The woman I love more than anything."

Mellisande finished writing.

"I've written down what you said. Read it back to me."

He took the paper from her. "I cannot read this. I only understand printing."

"Of course." She printed the note for him.

He read it haltingly, careful of the words he spoke.

"My darling, Lena. I'm sorry for the pain I caused you when I accused you of being no different than my mother or yours. I know now that you are just Lena.

You are yourself nothing more and nothing less. You are the woman I love."

"Add forever." He pointed to the last sentence. "The woman I will love forever. Then write, I hope you will forgive me and find it in your heart to take me back."

Mellisande added the sentences he wanted, and John made a few other changes, as well. When he finally got the note the way he wanted it, he printed it out himself. Many of the words he'd never written before and Mellisande helped him with the spelling.

Once he'd written the letter, he accepted the bottle of sand and an envelope from Mellisande. He wrote *To Lena* on the front.

"Now John, I hope you won't take this the wrong way, but when we get to New York, I'd like you to try on Robert's clothes. I believe they will fit you." She cocked an eyebrow and raked him from head to toe. "You need a new wardrobe.

"Won't it be difficult for you to see me in Robert's clothes?" He knew his suit was ill fitting. He'd had a difficult time finding one even this big. Though he didn't want to wear Robert's clothing, he would do anything to win back Lena and have her see him in a positive light.

"No. I don't think so. I'm glad they will go to you. He had impeccable taste, and you should benefit from his knowledge."

"Thank you for everything. I don't know what I would do without your help."

"Now we will see if the effort is enough for Helena. She has had two-and-a-half months to get over you."

John cringed when he heard the elapsed time. "I know. I'm hoping you're right and that she loved me, still loves me."

"I hope so as well. But we'll see, John. We'll just have to wait and see."

***

*E*ric arrived in New Orleans and discovered John Thorpe and Mellisande DuBois were leaving to travel to New York. His opportunities to be rid of Thorpe diminished with every passing day. He'd tried and failed.

Now the situation appeared to have changed again. What he thought would never happen, had. Thorpe and Mellisande were working together. At least, Eric assumed they were, since both were in Mellisande's private rail car headed to New York. He'd been able to get tickets on the same train at the last moment.

He thought of undoing the coupling holding the car to the train, only to find theirs was the first passenger car not the last as was the standard.

He was given no choice. Now he had to kidnap Helena and lure Thorpe into a trap. That was the only way he could get rid of both of them at once.

When he reached New York City, Eric hailed a cab outside the station and hurried to the mansion he'd called home for almost all his life. He knew that Vickers would let him in. The butler had always had a soft spot for Eric. He'd get the mansion if his plan worked.

He arrived there in short order and before Mellisande and Thorpe. He knocked on the door. The door opened and a large, bald black man in a black suit with a white shirt and gloves greeted him, not Vickers as he expected.

"May I help you, sir?"

He decided he would act like he belonged there and just walk in. "Who are you? Where is Vickers?"

"I am Thaddeus, and I work for the owner of this home, Mrs. Mellisande Drummond."

She was not the owner. Eric was the rightful owner. He stepped forward to enter.

The man put a hand on Eric's chest.

"What is your name, sir? You cannot enter unless you are on my list."

"What? How ridiculous. I've lived here my entire life."

"That may be true, sir, but you don't live here now. Your name please."

"Eric Rappaport."

The large man narrowed his eyes and crossed his arms over his chest.

"You, sir, are on my second list. The do-not-enter list. It contains only one name—yours."

Eric stamped his feet and clenched his fists.

"Why can't anything work out for me?"

"Perhaps, sir, because you've not earned it."

With those words, the butler stepped back into the house and closed the door.

Shoulders slumped, stomach knotted, Eric returned to his cab and gave the driver the address of his apartment. He had to find a way to pay his creditors or they would break his kneecaps, assuming they didn't just kill him outright.

CHAPTER THIRTEEN

ohn sat in the carriage across from Mellisande and wiped his hands on his pants. He hoped the plan he and his mother-in-law worked out would win back his wife.

They'd had a lot of time to get to know one another on the trip from New Orleans. They'd arrived at Grand Central Station five days after beginning their journey. During that time John and Mellisande shared their lives.

Mellisande told John about meeting Robert for the first time. She admitted that Robert helped her buy the business so he wouldn't have to share her with anyone. She was the one who decided to make the bordello a high-class establishment, with exclusivity available for a weekly fee.

Mostly what John learned was that Mellisande was a woman who loved her daughter fiercely, and he was lucky she was helping him rather than having her work against him.

The cab came to a halt in front of a stately mansion of red brick. Two white pillars held the cover for the porch. The cover itself was painted white, as were the shutters on the windows. The door was massive and made of dark wood.

Mellisande opened the door and walked into the foyer.

A large, bald-headed black man in a black suit with a white shirt and tie and wearing white gloves, greeted them. He broke into a wide smile.

"Mrs. Drummond. Welcome home."

"Thank you, Thaddeus. Where is my daughter?"

"Miz Helena is in the parlor, entertaining her suitors."

"What!" said John, his voice nearly a shout. His muscles went rigid, and he wanted to go into the parlor and tear every man there, limb from limb.

Mellisande laid her hand on John's arm.

"Calm yourself, John. We have our plan, and you must stick to it."

John fought his need to demand to see Lena and instead took a deep breath and gave Mellisande a curt nod.

"All right. I'm fine."

"Give me the letter you wrote," she instructed.

He reached into his coat pocket and handed her the envelope.

"Thaddeus," Mellisande handed the butler the letter. "Please hold this until I ring for you then you can take it to Helena. For now we are going to my room and get Mr. Thorpe ready. After that we will be in the library."

"Yes, ma'am."

Thaddeus turned and walked down the hall.

John and Mellisande took the staircase to the right and went to her bedroom. Dark wood dominated the room, in the dresser, bureau, four-poster bed, night-stands and desk. The drapes and walls were a pale blue color, the carpet blue-and-green oriental pattern.

He thought that nothing could come close to eclipsing that home in New Orleans, but this mansion was larger and even more lavish than the other house. This house made Mellisande's home look downright plain in comparison. John didn't know if he could ever get used to this kind of living.

"The closet is through that door." Mellisande pointed at the right wall. "You will find several dark gray suits. Try them first. If the first one you try on fits, then come out. Put on a white shirt and bring me the gray-and-red patterned cravat. I will tie it for you."

"What about my beard? I wanted to have it all shaved off for Lena. Now I've got a week's growth."

"It becomes you. The skin where your beard was is too white to be attractive. Keep the hair."

John went into the closet and saw probably fifty suits, black, brown, gray, navy, striped, and checked. He chose a gray suit with a small pinstripe, took off the ill-fitting black suit and put on Robert's. The garments fit perfectly. He'd never felt as good, as confident as he did in this suit. He found the red-and-gray tie Mellisande wanted and walked out of the closet.

"Ah, John, that is much better." She smiled and put her hand to her chin. "You look very nice." She gestured for him to turn around. "The clothes fit you as well as they did my Robert even across the shoulders. I thought they would. You are welcome to any or all of them."

Mellisande had him sit on the bed, while she stood between his legs and tied the cravat around his neck.

"Do I look all right?" He hated the need that came through in his voice, but this was important. This was as much for Lena as for him, to show her he'd changed.

"You look exquisite. Helena will be very pleased. Shall we go?"

"Yes."

John followed Mellisande to the library. Just outside the room, they saw Thaddeus. Mellisande nodded at him. He turned and entered another room down the hall.

John had thought Mellisande's library in New Orleans was large, but it didn't compare to this one. On his left, the entire wall was covered with bookshelves, each one filled from the floor to the ceiling. To his right, a large fireplace dominated the wall and a portrait of a man with dark hair graying at the temples hung above the mantle. Directly in front of him the view to the garden was unobstructed by a wall of any kind being entirely made of glass. He'd never seen, much less imagined, a place like this could exist.

"That is Helena's father."

Mellisande pointed at the painting.

"He sat for it just before he died."

"I'm sorry for your loss. I know you loved him very much."

She nodded and let out a long sigh. "I miss him so."

The door opened, and Lena entered like a whirlwind.

"What's the meaning of this?"

She waved the letter she held in her hand.

John turned to face her. He could only gaze at her beautiful face. He'd missed her so much.

"I thought it self-explanatory."

"Did my mother write this for you?"

"I would not do such a thing, *my petite,*" said Mellisande. "What you have is between you. As a matter of fact, I shall go and rid the house of the fortune hunters courting you."

"No, she did not," said John. "They are my words and I mean every one of them."

"How can you do this to me?" Her eyes were bright with unshed tears as she walked to the fireplace. "I've spent the last two-and-a-half months trying to forget you. Why did you come now?"

His thoughts whirling, heart pounding in his chest, he walked forward and stopped about six feet from her, his gaze never leaving her rounded stomach.

"You're expecting? How long were you going to keep it from me? Until after the divorce? Or had you planned not to tell me at all?"

"What difference does it make? You made your feelings about me quite well known."

She stopped, her chest heaving after the expression of her ire.

"So, I did."

He stormed past Mellisande, out of the room, out of the house and down the walkway. He didn't know what direction he would go, only that it was away from there. At the end of the walkway he stopped. He'd traveled across the country to win Lena back, and now she carried his baby. After all that happened, could he really blame her for her actions? John turned and re-entered the house.

*E*ric watched from the end of the driveway. He was dressed in all black, including his shirt, so he'd be harder to see in the dark. Unfortunately, to be safe, he knew he should wait until everyone had left before he entered the house, even through the secret entrances. But he didn't know when or if they would be leaving. He knew the mansion like no one currently in residence ever could, every entrance and secret passage.

The mansion was old, and the Drummond who built it, Robert's grandfather, had been a little batty. He trusted no one except his son. He had passages built in between the master and mistress suites so he could watch his wife without her knowing. Listen to her talk to her maid or tell her secrets to the walls, not knowing the walls had ears. Secret passages led from the garden outside the library to almost every room in the house.

When Eric was a boy, he came across the plans for the house and saw the secret passageways. He used them to spy on his mother and Robert. Or when Eric had done something wrong and Robert found out, Eric used the secret passages to get to his bedroom before his stepfather. Appearing ever innocent for how could he be in two places at one time?

Now, however, he would use them to get rid of Helena, Mellisande, and John Thorpe. He thought he should do John first, as he would be the hardest.

From his vantage point, he saw John stomp down the walkway, anger fairly rolling off the man. Something had happened in the first few minutes he'd been in the house to send him fuming from the mansion. Then he stopped, turned and went back inside. Apparently, he had a change of heart.

He'd wanted to wait until dark to go inside, but Eric needed to find out why John had been so angry. Perhaps he could use that anger to his advantage.

Eric stuck close to the hedge as he walked up the driveway and then ducked into the back garden. From there he went to the library's glass window. He pressed two separate bricks in order and a door swung open. A kerosene lamp hung on the wall just inside, and Eric lit the lamp before closing the door behind him.

He walked along the corridor lighting the wall sconces as he went, until he reached a set of steps. At the top he could either keep to the path he was on or turn to the right. The corridor straight ahead led to the master suite and the path to the right to the rest of the bedrooms on this floor.

Eric turned right. He came first to the mistress' suite. He peered in through the peephole in the door. Mellisande and Helena were there. Helena lay on the bed and Mellisande sat next to her. All he had to do now was wait for Mellisande to leave.

He didn't have to wait too long. She got Helena settled and then left the room. Eric waited for a while longer wanting to make sure Helena was asleep and wouldn't see him enter.

After about thirty minutes, he pulled on the wall sconce and the door in the wall swung open.

Eric unsheathed his knife, crept to the bed, and put his hand over Helena's mouth. Almost as soon as he touched her, he saw her eyes fly open. She apparently was a very light sleeper.

"Don't scream or move, Helena. I don't want to have to hurt you." He held up his knife, and the blade glinted in the waning light inside the room. "Do you understand?"

She nodded.

"I'm going to remove my hand now."

He pulled his hand from her face and held his knife at her belly. There was no mistake as to what he would do.

She remained silent, her hands crossed over her belly.

"Get up. You're coming with me."

"John will find you." She rose awkwardly from the bed.

"I don't think he will without my help. I saw him leave the house, rage consuming him."

"He just found out about the baby and was angry I hadn't told him, but he came back and got over his anger. You'll see. He'll come for you."

"That is what I want. I'm killing you both at the same time. Then I'll only have Mellisande standing in my way."

Eric took an envelope from inside his coat and laid it on Lena's pillow.

"You're insane, Eric. No court will make you the sole beneficiary of Robert's estate. The state will get the money before you do. I've made sure of that."

"What do you mean?"

They were in the passageway now lit with the light from the sconces and she walked in front of Eric.

"I made my plans clear in my will. If John and I don't survive, then the estate will go into a trust for our children. If there are no children," she placed a hand on her belly, "it will go to the Benevolent Fund for Widows and Orphans. I've directed them to build a new orphanage, staff it, and keep it running for the next twenty years."

"No, you haven't. You can't have been in the city long enough to have done what you say you did. I'm not a fool."

She remained quiet, and he knew he was correct. No changes had been made yet.

"Keep moving, Lena."

Coming upon a set of stairs she walked down them.

"Stop here."

Eric went around her and opened a door. It was twilight, seeing them would be difficult.

"Come now, we've a way to go."

She entered the garden.

He closed the door behind her.

She screamed.

Eric grabbed her, the knife back in his hand and at her throat.

"Do that again and I won't wait for John or Mellisande, and I'll start with your belly. Do you understand?"

She nodded.

He removed the knife and finished closing the door.

"No sense in letting anyone know how I got in."

"It won't matter how you got in. John will find you."

He laughed wickedly. "You wish he would find me. If and when he comes back, you and I will be long gone. Don't worry. He'll be in contact if he wants to see you again, that is. I left him a little note."

"You're setting a trap for him. It won't work." She suddenly realized Eric really was using her as bait for John. Part of her hoped he would find her, but she was also afraid that Eric would kill him if he did and she wouldn't be able to bear that. His dying would be her fault.

"You had better hope that's not true."

They left through the side entrance to the garden, which put them into an alleyway. Eric had her walk in front of him, occasionally prodding her with the knife.

"I'm moving Eric. I don't walk as fast now that I'm expecting." Lena hoped he believed the lie. She wasn't so far along that carrying the baby affected her walking at all. She was simply stalling for time.

At the end of the alley, she saw a carriage or a taxi. In the encroaching darkness she couldn't tell which.

They reached the conveyance, and she saw it was a taxi and her heart sank. There would be no finding her.

"Where are you taking me? Surely not to your apartment. So, where?"

"I have a small place outside the city. I used to keep my mistress there, until your father died, and she didn't want to be kept by a pauper."

She glanced up and down the street, looking for someone, anyone who could help her. "You were not a pauper. Ten thousand dollars a year is more than ten times what most people make, but you couldn't live on that could you? You borrowed against your supposed inheritance, didn't you? Of course, you did, you don't need to answer."

He kept his hand with the knife flat on her back while they walked side by side. Anyone who might see them would probably think they were out for an evening stroll.

"What would make you think that?"

"You're desperate. They must have come wanting their money when they heard Robert had died. You didn't take out reasonable loans with a real bank, did you? No, you took loans out from your bookies and the like. I'm surprised any of them let you live."

His mouth formed a thin line. "They can't get paid if they kill me, now can they. But they can hurt me a lot and I'd rather avoid that."

"Out of curiosity, how much do you owe them?"

"More than one hundred thousand dollars."

They reached the cab and he helped her into it. Once inside he replaced the knife in his boot.

Panic grew within her. She had to find a way to keep him from kidnapping her.

"You could sell the lodge and the apartment for more than that. Why don't you do that instead of doing this? You'd still have your annual income which is more than enough to live comfortably."

"Because, I want everything. I was supposed to get it all. All the money, the businesses, and the stocks, and bonds, the real estate, all of it was to be mine. Don't you understand? That's why I never said anything about you to your friends at school."

He smiled, the look of the devil in his eye.

"Oh, but wait. You didn't have any friends at school, did you?"

"I was shy. But you were such an evil piece of work, no one wanted to be around you."

"That was a long time ago."

"You haven't changed. You're still the same spoiled child you were then."

Eric reached across the coach and backhanded her.

"You will refrain from saying such things. As a matter of fact, you should probably stop talking all together. Don't make me gag you."

Lena had never been slapped before. Outraged, she put her hand on her burning face and nodded, knowing she had to hide her feelings.

They rode in silence for a while, just how long Lena couldn't say. The carriage came to a halt.

"Get out."

Eric didn't offer to help her down, not that she'd have let him if he had, but clambering awkwardly down the little steps to the ground was just another humiliation.

They were outside a small cottage. From what she could see, it was rather remote. She would have to figure out a way back to New York without a carriage.

Eric paid the driver and then was back beside her.

"Let's go. You can follow me now, there's no place for you to run."

He was right. She was safer with him as awful as that was to discover. Crickets chirped loudly and other animal noises she couldn't identify sounded around her. Lena followed him to the little house. He unlocked the door and walked in. She entered after he lit a lamp.

They entered the living room. A fireplace was on the left wall and a staircase on the right. Continuing past the living room was a dining room and then the kitchen. There were no doors between the rooms and none of them were large. All of the windows were covered with chintz curtains drawn closed. In the kitchen, a four-burner stove stood against one wall, a small table with four chairs stood against another with a door to the outside and directly across from her was a sink, icebox and counters with drawers below and cupboards above.

"Sit down, Lena. We'll be here a while before your husband finds my note. And if not him then Mellisande will find it. Either way one of them will come to rescue you and that's all I need. I can get rid of two of you at the same time."

"I won't cooperate." She crossed her arms over her chest and jutted her chin in the air. "I'm not letting you kill anyone else."

"Don't you understand? I have to." He paced to the sink and back to her then sat. "Now surely you want to try to survive, for that baby you carry. If one of them comes, I may change my mind and let you live."

She turned toward him. "I'm not a fool, Eric. I know you can't let me go. You want the money, but you'll never get it. Don't you understand? You were no blood relation to Robert. He has nieces and nephews that will inherit before you do."

"No." He slapped his hands flat on the table and stood. "That can't be true. I never met any family of his."

"They were estranged, but Robert has a sister, Carolyn Drummond Chase. Mellisande told me. I'm not lying. She was trying to get them to mend the rift."

"I don't believe you. Robert never talked about them. Now, I've had enough of your lies."

He approached her and took off his tie.

"No!" she shook her head vigorously. "Please I'll be quiet."

"It's too late for that."

He came around the back of her and tied the cravat around her mouth knotting it at the back of her head. The he took a length of rope and tied her to the chair.

"Now we wait."

The time passed slowly for Lena. Trussed up as she was, she couldn't warn anyone that Eric was armed. She'd seen the pistol in his belt while he bound her to the chair.

Finally, pounding came on the door.

John. He'd come for her.

"Come in, John."

The door slammed open.

"Where is she, Eric?" John called from the living room.

"Come on back and join us, why don't you?"

Eric released Lena and removed the gag.

"Stand up."

He pulled the gun out of his waistband.

"Stand up. Now."

Lena did as she was told.

Just as she stood, John's massive frame filled the doorway to the kitchen.

Her stomach was twisted in knots, but she'd never seen anyone so wonderful as John standing in that doorway. He'd come for her.

"Come sit down, John. Please join us."

"I don't want to sit."

"Ah, but I want you to sit, or I'll put a bullet in your lovely wife here. And her expecting and all...well that wouldn't be good now would it?"

John walked to the chair across from her and sat.

"Very good. Lena, take that rope and tie up your husband. Make sure he's tightly bound. If you don't..." he pointed the gun at her stomach.

Lena picked up the rope and walked to John.

"I'm sorry." She whispered. "I never meant for this to happen."

She wrapped the rope around him once. That's all it would go and still give her enough length to knot it.

"Don't worry. Have faith in me."

Hearing his words, a lump formed in her throat. "I've always had faith in you."

"Stop talking. Lena, come back over here. I want you to watch."

"No, please Eric. Don't do this. You won't achieve anything this way."

"They'll never catch me." He cackled.

Lena saw the insanity in him then and fear made her shudder. His eyes were wild but when he lifted the gun and aimed it at John, his hand shook.

He wasn't sure. She saw it. At that moment, she reached over and pushed him. The gun went off and hit John in the shoulder.

Lena screamed terrified John was dead.

Then John was there, free of his restraints. He wrenched the gun from Eric's hand, breaking his wrist with a snap. Next he threw a right punch at Eric, who fell, unconscious, to the floor.

"Oh, John."

Lena ran and wrapped her arms around him. So glad that the threat was over and John fought for her. But she shook, the events still sending a frisson of fear up her spine.

He put the gun in his coat pocket and then held her shielded in his embrace.

"He'll be out for a while. Let's go get the police. He's not going anywhere."

"You're wounded and bleeding."

"I'm fine. We'll get a doctor to patch me up when we get home."

John wrapped his good arm around Lena's shoulder after they got outside the cottage.

They walked to the cab John arrived in, whose driver held a large pistol in his hand.

"Take us to the nearest police station."

"Yes, sir." He waved his gun in the air. "Wasn't sure who'd be coming out, but I told you I'd wait, so I did."

"I appreciate that very much."

At the police station, John relayed the entire story, with Lena filling in the parts he didn't know.

The desk sergeant took down the statement and sent uniformed police officers to the cottage.

John and Lena stayed in the waiting area until the policemen returned. Eric was not with them.

"All we found was blood on the kitchen floor and on a rag by the sink."

"Damn. We should have tied him up." John looked at Lena. "Forgive my language. All I could think of was getting you out of that place."

"It's all right I can think of some colorful expletives myself."

He smiled at her. Then furrowed his eyebrows.

"I've never been so scared in my life as I was when I read his note. Yes, I read it all on my own, and then I took it to Mellisande. She wanted to come with me. I had to insist she stay at home in case additional correspondence from him arrived. Then when you pushed Eric, I was sure he would turn the gun on you and my heart stopped."

"You make it sound like you care for me."

She didn't want to read too much in his actions. Didn't want to get hurt again.

"I do care about you. I love you, Lena." He grasped her hand. "I didn't realize I did until I calmed down after I walked out, the first time. Then, tonight I was so dumb struck with anger that you would keep secret the fact of being with child. I'm sorry. I will control my anger. My intention is to never hurt you. I'm so sorry, Lena."

He loved her. Lena's heart soared. "I was sure you didn't love me, and I wasn't going to have you stay in the marriage just because I was having a child. That wouldn't be good for us or for the baby. That's why I didn't tell you."

"When I finally realized what an idiot I was tonight, I turned right around and came back. And then…oh Lena, I was so frightened." He squeezed her to him.

"I'm fine. I just want to go home and go to bed. With my husband. You know Eric will try again."

John moved a stray strand of hair behind her ear. "Yes, but now we know about the secret passages, and we can be prepared. We'll block them up."

"I don't think so. We need him to think we are still unaware of all the corridors. Then when he makes his move, you can apprehend him. We'll practice when we get home."

"We can hear him when he's in corridors. I thought it was mice in the walls. There was a distinct scratching sound and then the creaking of the door when it opened. I was just at the point between sleeping and waking to realize what was happening."

John took a deep breath.

"I'm glad you weren't hurt. That's all that matters."

"Speaking of being hurt, we need to get you home and get the doctor."

"The cab is waiting, let's go home."

CHAPTER FOURTEEN

They arrived home and found Mellisande waiting in the foyer for them. She immediately took Lena in her arms.

"I'm fine Maman. John is the one who is hurt. We need the doctor."

"You should have gone to the hospital," chided Mellisande.

"I wanted to get Lena home as quickly as possible. I'll be fine. It's just a scratch."

"Thaddeus!" called Mellisande.

"Right here, Mrs. Drummond."

"Go get the doctor, please."

"Yes, ma'am."

He hurried through the open door and out of sight.

"Come into the kitchen, let's clean that up so the doctor can see the extent of the wound."

Her mother gave orders just like a general in battle, leaving no room for argument.

The group reached the kitchen and Mellisande pointed at the table.

"Sit, John, while Lena and I get the needed supplies."

Lena filled a basin from under the sink with hot and cold water until it was just warm. Robert had put hot water in as soon as the first water heaters came out. It was a luxury Lena had definitely become used to.

She brought the basin to the table.

Mellisande dipped a washcloth in the water and rung it out.

"Take off your shirt, please."

John unbuttoned his shirt but found that he couldn't get the garment off the wounded shoulder. He'd lost more blood than he thought. Lena helped him remove the shirt.

Lena's mother cleaned the wound.

"You have two wounds one in front and one in back meaning the bullet probably went through you. That should be a good thing."

"That would be for me to decide, Mrs. Drummond. I'm Dr. Casey. Sean Casey."

Thaddeus had entered the kitchen with the doctor following closely behind.

The doctor was a man about Mellisande's age. He was of average height, which was still several inches taller than her and quite handsome with dark blond hair and sparkling green eyes.

"As you wish, Dr. Casey."

Mellisande stood away from John as the doctor moved in.

He set his bag on the table, took the washcloth from her, and cleaned the seeping blood off the wound.

"In this case, Mrs. Drummond appears to be correct. The bullet did exit your shoulder. I'll need to sew both wounds shut." The doctor took a bottle of medical alcohol from his bag. "I noticed that you have a nice bottle of Jameson's whiskey there, but I'll use the alcohol I brought. No need to waste good Irish whiskey. I'll pour it in the wound. The alcohol will help to clean the injury from the inside."

He poured the liquid into the wounds.

John grimaced and squirmed in the chair. His breathing was heavy, but he didn't make a sound. When the doctor was done, John took one big breath and then breathed normally.

"Now that it's over, I can safely say, I hope to never go through that again."

The doctor wrapped John's shoulder and arm so he couldn't move the upper part.

"Would you care for a whiskey, Dr. Casey? I have it on good authority that Jameson is a good brand." Mellisande almost purred the words.

Lena smiled. Her mother clearly liked the good doctor.

"It is the best whiskey money can buy," said the doctor as he packed his instruments into his bag. "And I'd like very much to take you up on your offer."

"John and I are going to bed. He needs his rest."

Lena put his good arm over her shoulder and walked out of the kitchen. Her mother's throaty laughter followed them through the door.

On the second day, they finally emerged from the bedroom. They needed sustenance, and they also didn't want to be any ruder to her mother.

Mellisande was in the library sitting behind the large mahogany desk. She looked up when they entered.

"Ah, I wondered if I should send someone in to see if you were still alive, but *mais oui*, I can see that you are both glowing."

"Mother." Heat rose in her cheeks.

"Helena, such talk cannot leave you embarrassed any longer, surely. You are, after all, a married woman."

"They are not discussed in polite society," said Lena

"We are not in polite society. We are in my home and we can discuss whatever we desire with impunity."

"Maman, we do not wish to talk about what we've been doing for the last two days. Suffice it to say, we've done a lot of talking and have decided to stay married. I will have Jacob take care of that."

"Already, done," said Mellisande. "I sent him a message yesterday. He will have the judge come here for the ceremony."

"Ceremony?" asked John, his brows furrowed. "I don't understand."

"My darling," said Lena, she reached out and took his hand. "Our marriage was not valid. When I became legitimate, when Robert and Mellisande married, my name changed, and I was Helena Drummond not

DuBois. Therefore, when we married and I didn't use my real name, our marriage was invalid. According to everything I and Jacob have read, I must use my legal name. Now, I ask you, will you marry me?"

John lightly squeezed her hand and hesitated just a moment, enough for her to think perhaps he'd changed his mind. Her heart began to pound.

"Yes, I will marry you. The sooner the better. It would appear we were living in sin, and I don't want our child to be a bastard. Mellisande, how could you know we would want to stay married, as the case is?"

"When you stayed, and she didn't throw you out the first night, I knew. There was no way my daughter would stay with a man she did not wish to be married to. My only questions are where do you plan on having the baby? And where are you going to live?"

"We're staying here," said John.

"We're moving back to Homestead Canyon," said Lena at the same time.

They looked at each other and laughed.

"I guess we have yet to figure that one out, but as soon as we do, we'll let you know, Maman," said Lena.

"Why not live in all places?" said Mellisande. "You could live in Wyoming in the spring and summer, New York in the fall and New Orleans in the winter."

Lena looked up at John. "What do you think, my love?"

"If that is what you want, then that's what we'll do. For now, we'll stay here in New York." John wrapped an arm around his wife's shoulders. "At least until the baby comes, and then we'll decide what to do after that. I need to send a telegram to Peter and let him know that I won't be back and to get another blacksmith."

"You only have a few months. *Mon petit-fils* should be here in January. Perhaps you'll have a New Year's *bebe*," said Mellisande.

"Perhaps. Maman. Perhaps. Would that make you happy?" asked Lena as she leaned into John's side.

"Whenever the *bebe* decides to make his entrance will be fine with me."

"You don't mind becoming a grandmother?" asked John.

"Mind? I'm ecstatic. I'll be able to spend time with this little one that I couldn't with Helena."

"You are of course welcome to stay with us wherever we happen to be for as long as you like... or until you and I want to kill each other," said John with a wink.

Mellisande winked back.

They all laughed.

---

*E*ric couldn't wait any longer. He'd been listening to the conversation in the library. She couldn't be allowed to have that baby. If there was a child, he'd never get his hands on that money. First, he had to get rid of John. He was the most difficult one. Being shot hadn't even slowed him down, and Eric needed to do it sooner rather than later. Now would not be too soon.

Tonight, when everyone was sleeping, he could slip in and out of the bedroom without anyone knowing. Now, how to kill him? The only way was to shoot him. If Eric got too close, Thorpe could easily overpower him as he'd done before.

But the shot will wake Helena and maybe the rest of the house. ARRGG! Why can't anything ever be easy?

He'd use ether. The ether would make John unconscious, so that Eric could smother him with the pillow.

That night, Eric entered the mistress' bedroom and approached the bed. Only one person laid in the bed— Lena. And she had her eyes open.

"We've been waiting for you Eric."

He narrowed his eyes. "I forgot you knew about the secret door."

"Too bad you won't be using it again."

"Where is John? I don't want to hurt you yet, so just tell me where he is."

She looked over his shoulder and smiled.

"He's right behind you."

Eric whirled. "What?"

John's fist landed in the middle of Eric's face, and he went down to the floor like a house of cards.

Relief surged through Lena and she jumped out of the bed and ran to John.

He put his right arm around her shoulders and brought her close, his left arm still bandaged from the shot a few days ago.

She leaned her head on John's chest. "I'll send Thaddeus for the police. They'll take care of Eric."

The man in question was coming to on the floor, holding his nose.

"You broke my nose."

Blood flowed from it.

John towered over Eric who sat on the floor. "You threatened to kill me and then would have killed my wife."

"It wasn't personal." Eric pulled his handkerchief from his pocket and held his head back to stem the flow of blood. "The money was mine, and you were in the way."

His calm demeanor belied the insanity Lena knew lay beneath.

"Maybe if, you'd have asked you might have gotten a loan," said Lena.

John looked at Lena. They both shook their heads.

Mellisande appeared in the doorway to the bedroom. "No. That is unlikely. You killed Robert. I had the liquor you gave him every night tested and high levels of arsenic were found in the bottle. Robert knew of your debts and your bequest was enough to settle your financial matters. You were greedy, Eric. That's all. Just plain greedy."

"I should have been his heir." He shouted as he brought his hand away from his nose and blood ran down his face. He seemed not to care. "I was the one who put up with you all these years. I'm the one that Robert talked to about how much he loved you and he wanted to marry you." He jutted out his chin and moved his head from side to side. "He needed to die."

Mellisande came forward to Eric, bent over and slapped his face sending blood flying. Her chest heaved and she said, "You are the one who needs to die."

Thaddeus knocked on the door.

"The police are here, Mrs. Drummond."

She backed away from Eric, out of his reach. "Thank you, Thaddeus. I don't know what I'd do without you. Please show them up."

The butler nodded his head and disappeared.

A few moments later, an older man appeared at the entrance to the bedroom.

"Mrs. Drummond," said the policeman. "I'm Captain Richards from the twelfth precinct. We can take it from here. I appreciate it if you would all come down to headquarters tomorrow and give your statements."

Lena watched as Mellisande eyed the captain. He was a handsome man with no ring on his finger. He had dark hair and silver at the sides, like Robert and appeared to be as robust as Robert had been. The ideal situation would be if her mother could find love again, perhaps with either Dr. Casey or Captain Richards. Lena smiled.

"What are you smiling at?" asked John as he looked down at her.

Lena nodded toward Mellisande.

"What? What about your mother?"

"Shh," Lena whispered. "She's interested in the

police captain. Perhaps we can have him to dinner… to discuss the case, of course."

"Of course," agreed John softly.

Two policemen hauled away Eric, bloody nose and all.

The captain walked over to Mellisande.

"We'll get back to you, Mrs. Drummond."

"Thank you, Captain. I look forward to it."

Mellisande extended her hand to the man.

"As do I," he said, before bringing her hand to his lips and kissing the top.

Her mother blushed prettily.

Lena was pleased.

After all the policemen left, Lena turned to her mother.

"I think we can all sleep better now that Eric is behind bars."

"I'm sorry about Robert," said John to Mellisande.

"So am I, but life goes on, and Robert would be the first one to say so. You children go to bed now and get some rest."

"What are you going to do?" asked Lena.

"I'm going into the library and having a brandy. It is some I brought with me from New Orleans and quite good."

"Do you mind if we join you, Maman? Though I think I'll have tea."

"Of course not." Mellisande swept an arm toward the door. "Shall we?"

After they'd each had a couple of drinks, everyone was more relaxed and ready for bed.

"I must say goodnight, Maman."

"Of course, *cherie*. Sleep well."

"I will."

Lena took John's hand.

He looked at her and then over at Mellisande.

"Yes, I need to get my wife to bed. I don't want all this commotion to affect the baby."

Mellisande came forward and kissed them on both cheeks as was customary in France and New Orleans.

"Good night. I think I'll stay up a while longer."

She glanced over at the portrait of Robert.

"I have things to think through."

As she and John left the room, Lena thought her mother was probably going to 'talk' to Robert about the police captain and the doctor. Her mother was definitely drawn to them both.

"I hope Maman can find love again. Love like ours. I've told you I love you, haven't I?

"I don't know that you have." He shook his head. "But I know anyway. I love you, too."

"I know you do. Even though you took a long time to realize it."

"You had to leave me before I knew what I had lost. Please don't ever put me through that again. The not knowing if you would take me back... God, I lost my world when I lost you."

Lena heard a roughness in his tone that brought a

lump to her throat. She reached up and stroked his cheek.

"But everything is all right now. We love each other, and what came before doesn't matter. We have now, and the future, and our baby. That's all I care about."

John swept her into his arms.

"John." She laughed as she put her arms around his neck.

"I want to show you how much I love you, and you walk too slowly."

Her laughter followed them to the bedroom and could be heard until he shut the door, cocooning them in their own little world.

---

*O*ne month after he watched Eric be arrested for trying to kill John a second time, John stood in the front of a church waiting for Lena.

Mellisande had begun seeing Captain Richards on a regular basis, and he was filling in for Robert to walk Lena down the aisle and give her hand in marriage to John.

The organist began to play. John turned and looked toward the back of the church.

Mellisande walked down the aisle, looking like an angel in a gown of yellow silk. Following her came Lena on the arm of Captain Richards. He wore his dress uniform and looked quite handsome, according to Lena.

Lena had placed her hand on his arm. She wore a

pale pink silk dress with a high waist to accommodate her expanding tummy.

She and the Captain walked slowly down the aisle, but finally she put her hand in John's and together they turned to face the reverend.

"Dearly beloved," he began.

Lena's eyes filled with tears. This time she was marrying the man she loved not some unknown stranger. She gazed up at her husband and found he was looking down at her with tears in his eyes, too. Her big strong husband as moved as she was by the ceremony that would unite them forever.

"Do you Helena Marguerite Drummond, take this man to be your lawfully wedded husband, to have and to hold for better, for worse, for richer, for poorer, in sickness and in health and to keep thyself only unto him, until death do you part?"

"I do." She said in a whisper, unable to speak past the lump in her throat.

"Do you John Wilfred Thorpe, take this woman to be your lawfully wedded wife, to have and to hold for better, for worse, for richer, for poorer, in sickness and in health and to keep thyself only unto her, until death do you part?"

"I do."

"John, repeat after me," instructed the reverend.

"With this ring, I thee wed." He placed a gold band with diamonds all around on her finger. This time it fit perfectly.

"Lena, it's your turn. Please repeat after me," said the reverend.

"With this ring, I thee wed." She placed a gold band with five diamonds set in platinum in the center of a ring of gold on his finger. One large stone in the middle surrounded by four smaller diamonds. This ring fit. It had been Robert's. Mellisande thought the arrangement appropriate that the ring that had been Lena's father's be now her husband's.

"I now pronounce you husband and wife. You may kiss your bride."

John wrapped his arms around Lena's waist as she placed hers around his neck. Then he lowered his head and took her lips in a sweet, chaste kiss.

When she felt him pull back, Lena tightened her hold on his neck. He then pulled her closer, careful of her belly, and straightened, taking her with him. Her feet hung in the air almost a foot off the ground as they kissed, wholly, completely. As always, she was breathless when they pulled apart.

"That's how I expect to be kissed every day," she whispered to him.

"And so you shall be," he whispered back. "With pleasure."

He set Lena on the floor.

Everyone in attendance—Mellisande, Captain Richards, and the entire staff and their families—clapped their approval.

EPILOGUE

February 22, 1888

John waited in the library for Mellisande to come with the news of the baby's birth. He went to the door opened it and listened but all he heard was his sweet Lena, screaming in pain. He quickly shut the door again, his jaw aching from keeping it clamped shut.

Mellisande had warned him of what would happen and so he was a little comforted to know this was natural.

On his last trip to the door, he opened it and saw his mother-in-law descending the stairs. He ran out of the room and went to her.

"Lena? Is she all right?"

"Mama and *bebe* are fine and waiting for you to join them."

"Is it a boy or a girl?"

"I'll let you see for yourself. Go now."

She waved him away toward the stairs.

John took the steps two at a time and ran down the hall to their bedroom. He stopped and collected himself before entering, wiping a hand over his hair.

"Lena?"

"Come in, sweetheart. We're ready for you."

He looked in the door and saw the smile on her face. Assured she was well, he approached the bed.

Lena held a baby in her arms.

The infant, happily chewing on its fist, looked red and bald.

As he got closer, he realized that the child had hair like its mother, blond so light as to look invisible on the baby's head.

"What do we have?"

"We have a son. A beautiful son."

Smiling, she held the baby up to John.

He took the child, awkward at first, and then becoming more confident. John's hands were so big the baby almost fit into one. A son. He had a son. Happiness filled him as he looked down at the tiny baby. He unwrapped the infant and counted all his toes and fingers.

"What shall we name him?" He looked at his son, who started to fuss. "I think he wants his mama." He handed the baby back to Lena.

She pulled the blanket over his toes "He probably wants to be covered up. It's too cold out here for him. As to his name, I thought we could call him Robert, after my father, and John, after you.

"I'm pleased with your choices and honored by them as well."

"Good. Now would you tell Mellisande and the staff to come up? They are all family."

"Yes, they are. I'll get them now."

Lena's mother, Thaddeus, three maids, and the cook all filed in to see the new addition to the family.

"He's beautiful," they all exclaimed.

"Let me hold my grandson."

Mellisande came forward and took the baby from his mother's arms.

"What have you named him?

"Robert John Thorpe."

"Your father would be pleased."

Her eyes filled with tears as she looked at her new grandson.

After a few minutes and being passed around to every person in the room, Robert was back in his mother's arms and crying. The little mews made Lena smile, even though she knew they would last only a short while before coming full-out crying when he was hungry or needed changing.

"It is time to feed Robert now, if you all wouldn't mind leaving."

"Of course." Thaddeus rounded up the maids and the cook, and they left to perform their duties.

"I'll leave as well," said Mellisande. "The three of you should be alone together, for now."

Lena watched everyone leave.

John closed the door behind them and then turned to his family.

She opened her nightgown, bared her breast, and brought the baby close. He took several tries before beginning to suckle.

"He's so small," mused John.

Lena chuckled. "Everyone is small compared to you. Mellisande assures me he is the normal size for a baby."

John leaned down and kissed Lena on the forehead.

"Thank you for my son and for being my wife. You've made my life complete."

She smiled up at him. "I love you, too."

Lena couldn't imagine being happier. She had a husband who loved her for herself, a home and family she had never thought possible just a year ago.

Life was good.

THE END

ABOUT THE AUTHOR

Cynthia Woolf is an award-winning and best-selling author of fifty-five historical western romance novels and six sci-fi romance novels, which she calls westerns in space. Along with these books she has also published five boxed sets of her books. The Tame Series, Destiny in Deadwood, The Marshals Mail Order Brides, Centauri Series and Swords and Blasters.

Cynthia loves writing and reading romance. Her first western romance Tame A Wild Heart was inspired by the story her mother told her of meeting Cynthia's father on a ranch in Creede, Colorado. Although Tame A Wild Heart takes place in Creede that is the only similarity between the stories. Her father was a cowboy, not a bounty hunter, and her mother was a nursemaid (called a nanny now), not the owner of the ranch.

Cynthia credits her wonderfully supportive husband Jim and her great critique partners for saving her sanity and allowing her to explore her creativity.

STAY CONNECTED!

Newsletter

Sign up for my newsletter and get a free book.

Follow Cynthia

https://www.facebook.com/cindy.woolf.5
https://twitter.com/CynthiaWoolf
http://cynthiawoolf.com

ALSO BY CYNTHIA WOOLF

Heart Wish series

Heart of Stone

Heart of Shadow

Heart of Silver

Bachelors and Babies

Carter

Cupids & Cowboys

Lanie

The Brides of Homestead Canyon

A Family for Christmas

Kissed by a Stranger

Thorpe's Mail Order Bride

The Marshal's Mail Order Brides

The Carson City Bride

The Virginia City Bride

The Silver City Bride

The Eureka City Bride

Bride of Nevada

Genevieve

Brides of the Oregon Trail

Hannah

Lydia

Bella

Eliza

Rebecca

Charlotte

Amanda

Emma Rose

Nora

Opal

Brides of San Francisco

Nellie

Annie

Cora

Sophia

Amelia

Brides of Seattle

Mail Order Mystery

Mail Order Mayhem

Mail Order Mix-Up

Mail Order Moonlight

Mail Order Melody

Brides of Tombstone

Mail Order Outlaw

Mail Order Doctor

Mail Order Baron

Central City Brides

The Dancing Bride

The Sapphire Bride

The Irish Bride

The Pretender Bride

Destiny in Deadwood

Jake

Liam

Zach

Hope's Crossing

The Stolen Bride

The Hunter Bride

The Replacement Bride

The Unexpected Bride

Matchmaker & Co Series

Capital Bride

Heiress Bride

Fiery Bride

Colorado Bride

Troubled Bride

The Surprise Brides
Gideon

Tame
Tame a Wild Heart

Tame a Wild Wind

Tame a Wild Bride

Tame A Honeymoon Heart

Tame Boxset

Centauri Series (SciFi Romance)
Centauri Dawn

Centauri Twilight

Centauri Midnight

Singles
Sweetwater Springs Christmas

Made in the USA
Monee, IL
07 July 2026

56546305R00134